MW01484080

THE LOOKOUT

A Gripping Survival Thriller

JACK HUNT

DIRECT RESPONSE PUBLISHING

Copyright (c) 2019 by Jack Hunt
Published by Direct Response Publishing

Copyright © 2019 by Jack Hunt

All rights reserved. Direct Response Publishing. No part of this book may be reproduced, scanned, or distributed in any printed or electronic form without permission. Please do not participate in or encourage piracy of copyrighted materials in violation of the author's rights. Purchase only authorized editions.

This Book is licensed for your personal enjoyment only. This Book may not be resold. If you would like to share this book with another person, please purchase an additional copy for each person you share it with. If you're reading this book and did not purchase it, or it was not purchased for your use only, then you should return to an online retailer and purchase your own copy. Thank you for respecting the author's work.

The Lookout: A Gripping Survival Thriller is a work of fiction. All names, characters, places and incidents either are the product of the author's imagination or used fictitiously. Any resemblance to actual persons, living or dead, events or locales is entirely coincidental.

ISBN: 9781651827314

Also By Jack Hunt

The Renegades
The Renegades 2: Aftermath
The Renegades 3: Fortress
The Renegades 4: Colony
The Renegades 5: United
Mavericks: Hunters Moon
Killing Time
State of Panic
State of Shock
State of Decay
Defiant
Phobia
Anxiety
Strain
Blackout
Darkest Hour
Final Impact
And Many More…

Dedication

For my family.

Prologue

Kelly Danvers thought she was going to have a heart attack as she sprinted through the dark, empty streets of Emery. Her chest heaved, throat burned and knees pumped like pistons. How much of a head start had swinging that lamp bought her? Not enough. An angry shout filled the air behind her, he was on her tail, but he wouldn't catch her this time.

She kept going, wheeling around corners. To either side were high snowbanks, unplowed driveways and vehicles blanketed in snow. Lights flickered in the distance, shadows straining toward her. The downtown, where she needed to be was close yet still seemed too far away. Dismay filled her chest like a heavy weight. Logic told her to seek help from neighbors but they wouldn't believe her, and any delay could prove costly. No, the only way to stop him was to go to the top.

Let them see for themselves.

Then there would be no denying.

It was a little after 11 p.m. A change in weather punished the small Idaho town.

Her bare feet plunged into slush, numb from the cold. Her teeth chattered, and body shivered hard from wearing nothing more than a bikini. What little warmth gained from the hot tub was now gone, replaced by freezing temperatures. When a harsh wind blew in her face, she barely gasped — too cold to feel it. Not even snow could slow her or ease the pain coursing through her body.

This time she knew with certainty that he would have killed her.

A vehicle's headlights washed over her. Panic shook her to the core. *Is it you?*

She darted left, cutting through a yard, tears streaking

her red cheeks.

Please, God, please don't let him find me. Don't let it be him.

A silver SUV tore past her, splashing slush two feet high. She breathed a sigh of relief only to go tense at the sound of a vehicle, then his angry voice. "Kelly!"

Was he driving? On foot?

Did he know where she was going? Maybe he would try to cut her off before she got there. She wouldn't allow that. Kelly summoned strength she didn't even know she had as she staggered into another road. The world around her blurred behind a curtain of tears. She cut through a small wooded area, going on sheer instinct more than anything.

Disoriented when she exited the rear of her home, she'd gone southwest. A change of direction, the tiniest miscalculation and she could find herself lost in the surrounding evergreen forest. Gnarled tree branches slapped at her chest. Thorns and brambles raked her legs. She screamed but nothing came out except a croak.

That's exactly what he wanted.

Don't have a voice. Don't answer back. Don't get out of line.

Trapped.

It had been her life for far too long.

Bursting out of the tree line, she stumbled to her knees with nothing to hold.

The shock of hitting the ground brought more tears to her eyes.

Scrambling, she pressed on at the sound of a vehicle getting closer.

This was him. He'd seen her. Any minute now he would scoop her up.

She squinted into the blackness of night trying to get her bearings.

Her eyes scanned the terrain, looking for landmarks, anything to indicate where she was. A sign for a hardware store, a poster for an event at the café in town.

It wasn't far now.

A shot of adrenaline made her realize she had more gas

in her tank. She stumbled across the slick, cold street. A few bundled-up pedestrians looked over and frowned, then smiled, unaware, confused even. They must have thought it was a prank.

There.

She squinted.

In The distance.

Looming out of the snowy night, a beacon of light.

The low-slung white building crouched at the corner of the street, an American flag at full mast, flapped in the breeze. Beyond that a police SUV smothered in white powder, and a pale yellow light emanating from the windows.

Soaking wet, frozen to the bone, Kelly shouldered the door and collapsed inside the warmth of the lobby. Behind thick plexiglass, a blurry image of an officer scrambling toward the door. A low buzz blasted from hidden speakers before a thick door swung wide. A second later, the officer dropped down beside her as she regained consciousness.

"Ms. Danvers? What happened? Who did this?"

"It was him," the words barely came out, pushing past a damaged voice box, almost inaudible. "He attacked me."

She squinted through a swollen eye.

"Help!" the male officer shouted over his shoulder before scooping her up in his strong arms and carrying her through the doorway into an office of desks covered by computers, phones and paperwork. She groaned as the world spun around her. "I've got you. Hang in there." She heard footsteps, someone gasped and the officer shouted for them to swing the cruiser around. He was going to take her to the hospital immediately.

Eyes bloodshot, dipping in and out of consciousness, struggling to breathe, Kelly could feel her life drifting away.

"Give me a name. Who did this?"

"He did…"

"He? Who? Who are you referring to, Ms. Danvers?"

His name, his voice, his twisted face looming over her,

a look of uncontrollable anger. A flash of violence as if he was right there about to finish what he'd started. Words escaped her lips but they came out as a mere whisper, nothing more than a breathless rasp. The officer placed his ear to her mouth and she repeated, "My husband, Deputy Cole Johnston."

Chapter 1

Something bad was about to happen.

When Kelly saw the road sign that let her know she was five miles from Emery, her breath turned shallow and her pulse sped up. She couldn't shake the sense of dread as the taxi rumbled toward the outskirts of town.

Three weeks.

Three weeks had passed since that fateful night and her hands still trembled, though now she wasn't sure if it was from returning or the second cup of java she'd had that morning. She tried to shrug off the oppressive feeling and bask in the frozen beauty outside but her anxiety was getting worse the closer she got.

It was clear that Friday in northern Idaho during the last week of December. Temperatures had plunged to four degrees above zero and the evergreen trees were covered in a heavy layer of snow. From inside the warmth of a taxi that smelled musty, Kelly looked absently out the frosted window, lost in thought as her phone began buzzing. She fished into her bag and the name and face of her literary agent, Nora Green, appeared on the caller ID. She groaned and contemplated not answering as she knew where the conversation would go and reliving it was not how she wanted to start the day. Still, three years and she knew Nora well enough to know she was like a dog on a bone. Kelly was aware that unless she turned off the ringer, the calls would continue for the remainder of the day like a telemarketer that wouldn't give up.

She tapped accept and summoned a positive tone. "Nora."

"Kelly. Finally. I've been trying to get hold of you for weeks"

"Yeah… I changed my number, how did you—?"

"Your mother." Nora went silent knowing that Kelly preferred to keep her personal and business life separate. It was the one thing she had control over and she guarded it fiercely. Nora was quick to explain. "What? You haven't returned my calls, texts or emails. You'd practically disappeared off the face of the planet, and you are far too young to pull that reclusive writer bullcrap. What was I supposed to do?"

Kelly brought a hand up to her high cheekbone, and tucked a long strand of jet-black hair behind her ear. "Sorry about that. Ugh. I haven't exactly been in the mood for small talk."

There was silence, and Nora shifted down a gear. "I know. I heard. Your mother told me." A pause. "God, Kelly, I'm so sorry." She took a deep breath. "I mean it makes sense now. The missed deadlines. The lack of communication. You should have told me, hon."

"Would it have changed anything? The deadline would have still been there."

"Oh screw the deadline. I could have made some calls, rearranged things. It's the PR that I'm worried about. Fortunately your name wasn't attached to the news article on Cole but once it gets out that it was you, the media will have a field day." She sighed. "Which reminds me, how have you managed to keep it under wraps?"

"I haven't. You might want to ask the department about that. They haven't exactly been helpful."

Nora grumbled. "To be expected I guess. One of their own and whatnot. But he was arrested."

Kelly rubbed her eye; the new contact lenses were irritating her. "Of course he was, they didn't have a choice. He was slapped with an assault charge and an order of protection was issued against him. But it didn't exactly do much. They released him on his own recognizance."

"Released?"

"Yeah, they don't consider him a flight risk. History I guess; his position with the department has a lot to do with it."

"But he has a history of abuse, right? I mean, your mother said you told her that he'd hit you before?"

Kelly ran a hand around the back of her neck. She really didn't want to get into it. "Those times were not documented. This was the first time I…"

Nora went silent and Kelly could only imagine what

she was thinking, what anyone would think. Why hadn't she told someone earlier? Why hadn't she left him? She was a walking abuse statistic, a cliché, and it sickened her. The fact was who would have believed her? Cole was a familiar face in the county, in the schools and at public events. Hell, he'd helped raise money for kids with cancer. He was by all rights, a pillar in the community. Instead of getting into the past, she simply tried to bring the conversation to a close. "The case has been downgraded from a felony to a misdemeanor. Cole told them a different story and I guess..."

"They're taking his word over yours," Nora added.

Kelly shrugged and blew out her cheeks. "I don't know. I'm still waiting to hear back on the outcome of the arraignment. From what I heard, he pleaded not guilty and he was released. The department has placed him on administrative leave pending an internal affairs investigation. The case hasn't been dropped by any means but by the sounds of it, it's not exactly priority. Seems his lawyers think he has a strong case. What that is, I've yet to find out but I'm meant to chat with my lawyer this week so I will learn more then."

Kelly's conversation must have been the highlight of the taxi driver's day as he kept sweeping his rearview mirror and staring at her. Did he pity her? Think she was a joke? She still hadn't moved beyond what people thought. Since leaving Cole, she had vanished into obscurity, avoiding public places, staying low and thinking — overthinking.

"Well, keep me updated. I hope that bastard gets everything he deserves and more. Um… your mother said you were heading back to Emery today, is that right?"

"Yeah, I'm nearly there."

"Why?" Nora asked.

"I haven't put out a good book in over two years, Nora. I need to get back to it."

She laughed. "*A Call to War* spent a hundred and nine weeks on the *New York Times* Bestseller List — in the top three slots I might add — it was translated into over eighty different languages, won the Pulitzer Prize, has sold millions upon millions of copies and is now considered one of the Great American Novels of our time. The only authors that have come close to that are Harper Lee, and John Steinbeck. And I might add, Harper Lee didn't publish anything further for what... around fifty-five years? So... a good book? Please, Kelly, you underestimate yourself."

"You know what I mean."

"Listen, darlin'... I am all for hearing that you are ready to put your fingers on the keys again — trust me, the publishing world is waiting with bated breath after your last, but after what you've been through... do you really think it's the right time?" She waited for a response; Kelly didn't give one. "It's only been two years. I think people can wait another year for your next novel. Wouldn't it be best to stay with family until this is over? Besides, it's not like you're hurting for money." There was a pause. "Are you?"

Kelly managed to summon a chuckle. "I'll let you know once the lawyers have been paid." She took a swig of her coffee and continued, "No, look, I can't just sit around at my mom's place. I'll go out of my mind. Anyway, I've put it off long enough. If I don't get going now I don't think I'll ever write again."

"Oh, poppycock! I won't have you spiraling down into depression, drink and drugs. I already have enough clients like that."

Kelly chuckled. "Look, it's not the only reason I'm heading back — I have to head up to the peak and winterize the lookout for the season, so I might as well use the time to do some writing."

"You're still running that old place? I thought you'd sold that years ago."

Back when Kelly was an unknown writer, paying the bills and writing was a challenge, so as a means to support her career her father had purchased an old fire lookout tower for less than twenty grand with the goal of turning it into a rental property. It was an investment. They were to share in the profits. It had done well. Most months it was booked up but over the winter that was another story.

Her fascination with fire lookouts and their place in American history had started when she learned that Jack Kerouac had worked in one before he published *On the Road*. That's when the idea was born. Still, getting her hands on one was difficult. Since the first was erected back in 1905 to allow the Forest Service to spot fires, over four thousand had been in operation around the United States, mostly in National Forests. Eventually that number dwindled to less than nine hundred as new technologies such as air patrols and computerized lightning detection systems took over.

Prior to the purchase, only a few hundred were still actively being used by rangers. Of course this was the opportunity she was after. Kelly had scoured the internet until she found one that was only a few years old, located on sixteen acres of land just on the outskirts of the Idaho Panhandle National Forests. It was nestled deep in the evergreen woods, a remote off-the-grid location that was tricky to get to even in the summer months. Once it was purchased, the rest was history... and a lot of hard work, but it paid the bills and kept a roof over her head while she focused on writing.

"Yeah, I'm renting it out all year now."

Nora sounded skeptical. "People still use it in the winter?"

"Sure do. Hikers, hunters, couples wanting a cozy retreat. I don't get a lot of calls for it but that's fine. In fact this year will be the first time I've closed it up to the public. I figured I'd use it for my writing. You know, go up and get this next book completed."

"But you could have done that in Boise."

Kelly laughed. "I'd never get any writing done at my mother's. Too many distractions. And, well…"

"You know, hon, you could write anywhere. The Bahamas, for goodness' sakes. Somewhere warm, tropical, where you can drink a margarita beside the pool, and who knows… maybe even meet a decent man."

When Kelly didn't laugh, Nora said, "A little early. Sorry." It wasn't the first time she had put her foot in her mouth, Kelly was used to it. Nora was quick to shift away from the awkward moment. "Well at least please tell me you have someone staying with you."

"No. It's just me. I mean… initially."

Silence followed.

"After what you just went through?"

Kelly sighed. "I'm thirty-eight, Nora. A grown woman. And I'll be damned if I'm going to live in fear or put my life on hold one more day because of that asshole. No, Emery is my home and he's not running me out. If I choose to leave, it's because I choose. Besides, my brother said he might visit."

"Might?" Nora didn't sound too convinced. She acted like a second mother, protective and slightly overbearing. "Well you keep me in the loop, okay? And if you finish that novel, shoot it over."

"You'll be the first to read it, Nora. I promise."

* * *

Light snow had begun to fall as Kelly climbed out of the taxi that was now parked in front of the Mercantile gas station on Main Street. The garage beside it was wide open and a grease-covered mechanic in blue overalls was busy working beneath a sedan. He glanced her way for a second before continuing. The store was displaying ads for cigarettes, beer, hot dogs and lotto tickets. She was supposed to meet Hank Walton, her friend and current caretaker of the lookout. She thumbed off payment to the driver through the window before carting over her bags to a bright orange vehicle that would take her the rest of the way.

The Snowcat was an absolute beast, rugged, durable; a must-have for overcoming the deep snow that prevented regular vehicles from reaching her property. The only other way was using 4WD or a snowmobile in the winter season.

Three years ago, when she decided to keep it open in the winter, Kelly had searched for a way to transport guests up to the lookout, and a good friend had given her a tip about an ad posted online. It was perfect. The 1964 Thiokol Snowcat was a steal, a side project that required little more than refurbishing the inside with new seats, cozy blankets, heat and snowshoes for guests. A fresh lick of paint and it was ready to use. Although Snowcats were used more for maintenance than transportation, she couldn't help but think it was a worthy opponent for the peak's challenge. She was right. Not only did it get them there safely, it added to the experience.

Kelly threw her bag in the back just as Hank staggered out of the gas station, juggling a coffee, a muffin and a pack of cigarettes.

"I'll catch up with you later, Joe," he muttered to the owner as he jogged over, his mouth breaking into a smile. "Kelly. You made it."

"Hey Hank," she said warmly, wrapping her arms around the hulk of a man. Dark skinned, a full beard, short in stature, he wore a thick winter jacket, a red plaid shirt, jeans and yellow work boots. He was closing in on fifty, married and a staple sight in the community. When he wasn't transporting guests to and from the lookout, he did odd jobs around the town. "Good to see you."

He hugged her tight, gripped her shoulders and

addressed her like a parent. "How are you?" he asked with genuine concern. Since the event, Kelly had been able to distinguish two types of people. Those who cared, and those who pitied her.

If people asked how she was doing, she often shrugged and said nothing. *You want to know what it's like to come out of an abusive relationship?* She wanted to ask. *It feels like crap. Like someone has torn out your heart and soul and stomped on it.* But she never said that. Instead she would just say, as good as can be. When awkward silence followed, whoever had asked would just shift the topic back to themselves almost as if they knew they shouldn't have gone there.

Hank wasn't like that, so she replied. "You know…" she said, offering back a strained smile. He nodded and didn't take his eyes off her as if peering into her soul.

Truth be told, Hank was like a second father to her. Thirteen years they'd known each other. A local handyman, an I-can-do-everything kind of guy, she'd hired him to do work on the lookout.

Seeing an opportunity, Hank had offered to look after the place when she wasn't around, transport guests, haul in wood, do general maintenance and so on. At first she was a little hesitant to let go of the reins but as book tours, interviews and daily life took up more of her time, it just made sense to let him handle it. So far he'd done a great job.

Not one to probe into another's business, Hank gestured toward the Snowcat.

"Well, hop in. We need to get going." He glanced at his watch. "I told your friends I would be there half an hour ago."

"Erin didn't take her 4WD?"

"No, she wanted the whole Snowcat experience. You should have seen the two of them in the back. Like teenagers, they couldn't take their hands off each other." He glanced up. "Anyway, they're calling for a snowstorm, so I want to get back before dark."

She frowned, raising a hand to catch a few flakes. "It's just a little snow."

He sniffed the air. "Looks can be deceiving." She snorted as she climbed in the back. He was a walking barometer. She slammed the door closed, shutting out the frigid weather, and settled in for a warm but bumpy ride up to the remote peak.

Chapter 2

Kelly stepped out of the Snowcat at the base of the steep driveway and surveyed the sanctuary at the edge of the sky. They'd been driving for fifty minutes and it felt good to get out and stretch her legs. As she worked out the tension in her neck, she looked into the distance at the twenty-five foot tower of steel and wood which loomed over dense evergreen trees. Deep in the heart of logging country, at an elevation of around 4,800 feet above sea level, was the original 200-square-foot red wood cabin. Perched on top of metal stilts, it offered 360 degrees of breathtaking views.

"Well, tell your friends I'm here to take them back. I'll bring up the logs on the sled and drop back in a couple of days with some more as there wasn't much left from our supplier today. Seems one of the locals bought up a huge batch. You let me know if you need anything though." She nodded, hugged and thanked him. "Good to have you home, Kelly," Hank said.

Slipping into snowshoes, Kelly flung her bag over her shoulder and hiked up the steep quarter-mile driveway. It wasn't easy. She'd forgotten how tough off-the-grid living could be. In the summer, 4WD vehicles could go right up to the lookout but with the amount of snow that dumped, and the sharp turn on the driveway, it just made it impossible in the winter months. She breathed in icy cold air; her breath formed like a ghost before her as she trudged toward the peak. It was like entering a magical world, akin to a fairy tale. A flock of birds screeched overhead as a moose vanished into the surrounding snow-covered forest. The wildlife was abundant, with bears, deer and wolves — a frequent sight — and an ever-present danger.

"Erin. Bryce?" Kelly called out but got no response. She groaned, remembering her voice was still recovering. Since that night her throat felt like she'd swallowed gravel. Although she'd shut down the rental for the season so she could stay there, she'd told her best friend Erin

Miller that she could use it for a week. Erin was a hairdresser in Emery. She ran a hair salon just off Main Street, a thriving business that attracted clients throughout the county and gave her a finger on the pulse of new gossip.

Kelly's eyes washed over the clearing. Her sixteen acres of property spanned into the dense forest, leaving a small area that was taken up by the lookout and a small composting outhouse nearby. A long winding path that vanished into the forest led up to a large raised platform with a sunken firepit flanked by two Adirondack chairs. At the center was a large shed which had been converted into a wood fire sauna. On a clear day, you could just see it between the trees. It was one of the things she was most proud of as she'd been involved in renovating it from scratch.

She squinted through falling snowflakes to see if they were up in the cabin. Nope. No movement.

Kelly clamped shut the top of her long tweed jacket with one hand as she reached the bottom of the lookout.

Access to the above cabin was gained by climbing twenty-seven steps that led to a trapdoor.

Making her way up, she noticed the hatch wasn't locked which meant they had to be nearby as it was supposed to be sealed when not in use. She heaved the heavy door upward and clambered into the space. It was modest, uncluttered and practical, containing one queen bed covered by a thick duvet and a colorful horse blanket, a wood-burning stove off to the right, and cooler to the left of the bed for food and drinks. In addition to that were foldable stools, a foldable table, a sink, a portable butane burner, a grinder and Chemex coffee maker, along with as much storage and counter space as she could fit beneath the windows.

A small suitcase belonging to Erin lay open on the bed with clothes thrown in haphazardly. Two unwashed coffee mugs were on the counter, the garbage hadn't been emptied down the chute and the table was still folded out with stools beneath it as if used that morning.

Kelly set her bag down and opened the door that led

to the wraparound deck with a railing that was waist high. Large shutters that were supported by two beams of wood had been opened to let light in. In the winter she'd usually close them because too much snow would collect on top and she was worried the beams wouldn't hold and eventually the panels would crash into the windows. A hard gust of wind blew in and she took a moment to survey the area for any sign of them. Erin was meant to be looking after her German shepherd, Boomer. She figured they must have taken the dog for a walk. Far below, Hank unloaded logs from the sled and covered them with a tarp. He looked up and cupped a hand over his eyes. "They coming?"

She shook her head. "Must have gone out."

"You got enough wood?"

Glancing inside, below the counter, she saw that the area used for storing logs was almost empty.

"We could use some more."

He gave a nod and dragged the sled of logs up.

At the far corner of the deck was a pulley system she'd

installed which allowed her to haul up groceries, wood and anything too heavy to carry. Hank filled up the metal basket, along with some kindling, and Kelly yanked on the thick climbing cord until the basket was within reach.

No sooner had she taken the load into the cabin than she heard Boomer barking. Kelly turned to see the dog bounding into the clearing and greeting Hank. "Boomer, old boy!" Hank crouched only to be licked to death.

Erin emerged from the tree line, wearing a red down jacket, blue jeans, snowshoes and a light-colored wool ski cap which partially hid her shoulder-length bright pink hair.

It was easy to see why she became a hairdresser as Erin could talk the ear off a donkey and she had bucketsful of confidence. Not far behind her was her boyfriend, Bryce, a tall, rugged guy outfitted in warm winter gear with a stylish face mask. He tugged the material down, looked up and waved to Kelly as she stepped toward the railing. Kelly let out a whistle and Boomer's ears perked up. The dog instantly knew it was her and took off toward the lookout. Boomer had no problem climbing the stairs. She'd got him four years ago from a pound after someone abandoned him. Couldn't have asked for a better dog. Besides the times she had to go on book tours, the dog was always at her side. Erin had suggested she take Boomer while Kelly was recuperating with her mom as they'd both formed a strong bond and it would help her out temporarily.

He burst through the opening like a rocket.

Kelly dropped to her knees, a broad smile forming.

"Hey boy, miss me?" Boomer wagged his tail, his nails tapping against the wooden floor like rain. She ruffled the hair behind his ears, and under his chin and gave him a treat from her pocket before he calmed down.

Minutes later, Erin entered as Kelly was cleaning up. "Hey sweetheart." She paused. "Oh, I'm sorry, I was about to get to that."

"Ah, it's fine," Kelly said in a raspy voice, waving her off. "More importantly, did you enjoy yourself?" she asked.

Erin stared at her. "God, you sound awful."

It was like suffering from a bad cold but far worse, she could barely raise her voice beyond a croaky whisper. The remaining bruising to her neck was covered by a thick scarf. It was better that way. Having people stare only made her anxious.

Erin was unable to contain her excitement. She shot out her left hand and showed a large twinkling gem. "He proposed. Got down on one knee and everything."

"Oh hon, that's fantastic. Congrats," Kelly said giving her a big hug.

"Totally caught me off guard. I just thought we were going to have a week away, and…" She clenched her teeth together and beamed. "Anyway, we're planning for a summer wedding. You'll be my bridesmaid, won't you?"

"Of course. I would be honored."

Erin hugged her again and squealed in her ear.

"So where is the lucky man?"

"Ah, shooting the breeze with Hank, having a cigar." Erin smiled as she rolled her eyes. "You know, guy stuff."

She took a deep breath and then cocked her head to one side, the smile quickly fading. Kelly knew the look, and what question would come next so she answered before Erin asked.

"I'm fine."

Erin pursed her lips and squinted. "Really?"

"As good as can be."

Kelly took a seat at the folding table which displayed an old map of the area from the 1970s beneath glass. She took out of her bag some of the mail she'd had redirected to her mother's but hadn't got around to opening. One of them was from Cole. She'd considered tossing it but her lawyer had told her if he made contact to keep it as they could possibly use it against him if it contained a threat. She hadn't brought herself to read it. She figured it was just another ruse, a letter full of apologies, begging her to forgive him and come back. The apologies were empty, nothing more than a way to continue the cycle of abuse.

Erin placed a hand on her shoulder. "You want some hot cocoa?"

"Ah you don't need to."

Erin glanced out the window. "Well it doesn't look like the guy's in a rush."

Minutes later the metal kettle on the stove let out a whistle. Erin poured boiling water and brought her drink and placed it in front of her. Kelly nursed the cup, letting it warm her hands as Erin took a seat across from her. Erin had these big wide eyes like she was eager to tell Kelly all about her time at the lookout.

Instead, both of them glanced at Cole's letter.

"You seen him?" Kelly asked. Not that she cared but she was curious to know how he was handling the unsavory and humiliating news that had spread. In a town of just over eight hundred, rumors traveled fast, bad news even faster, and the local newspaper had been the first to carry the story.

She still had a copy.

Emery Police Officer Arrested for Allegedly Trying to Strangle Wife.

Allegedly, the choice of words sickened her.

Erin took a deep breath as she stirred her drink. "No but Bryce did, he said he saw him go into Charlie's Bar a couple of weeks ago. He was alone. Seems he's been drinking hard and flapping his gums." Erin couldn't hide her disgust of the man. "He's made a point to do the rounds and make it clear that he had nothing to do with it."

Kelly's eyebrows rose. "Nothing to do with it?" She shook her head before slowly bringing up a hand to her neck. Few people had seen the photos taken at the hospital on the night of the attack, or the ones after which looked even worse once the deep purple bruising appeared. Her eye was still sporting a shiner he'd given her. The gash on her bottom lip had healed over. The scratches were gone. In three weeks it had all faded considerably. Thankfully she was able to cover most of it with makeup but it was still there lurking beneath the surface.

Erin perked up, trying her best to keep the mood light. "So you're moving ahead with writing that next book?"

"Attempting would be a better word."

There was a pause.

"And when it's done. What then?"

"My mother wants me to move to Boise."

"And you?" Erin asked.

Kelly sighed and squeezed the bridge of her nose. "I don't know from one day to the next, to be honest, Erin. One moment I think it's a good idea, a fresh start, distance — and the next... I think otherwise and just get angry." She clenched her jaw. "Emery is my home. Or it has been for a long time. No matter what the outcome, the thought of leaving because of him in some way makes me think he's won."

Erin nodded. "Yeah, I hear you."

Tears formed in Kelly's eyes. "Yesterday I thought I could do it — you know, stay, but I don't know if I can. Even if they send him to prison, there are just too many bad memories here. Besides, I don't know if I'm... strong enough." She exhaled hard. "I mean, I should have done more, told someone, fought back or walked away sooner.

I didn't."

Erin reached across the table and placed a supportive hand on top of hers.

"You did walk away. It doesn't matter when, only that you did. Right? Look at you now. You had the courage to leave."

Kelly stared back at her through tears and nodded slowly. "But as long as I remain in Emery, I'm never really going to be free, am I? People talk. I'll always be that woman who was abused, that cop's ex-wife, that..." Kelly exhaled hard looking out the window, trying to control her emotions. "I don't want to be that, Erin. I just want to move on, forget that it ever happened. But how?"

Erin studied her.

"Screw what other people think. Okay? They don't have a damn clue. The ones that matter understand. We're here for you. Anything you need, we've got your back. You know that, right?"

Kelly nodded as tears rolled down her face. "I appreciate that, hon. I'm just scared. About everything.

The present, the future. That I won't trust anyone again. I'm scared I'll let the wrong person in." She pursed her lips. "I'm scared I'll wind up alone. Probably living with a house full of cats." She looked at Boomer and he cocked his head. "Alright. Dogs." Erin chuckled and then gave her a serious look.

"You're not alone. And don't ever think you're not strong, Kelly. What you did walking into the police station took guts. Being vulnerable is strength. Moving forward is strength. Don't let him have that part of you. It's the best part. You're stronger than you think. Just showing up here is proof of that."

Kelly pulled a tissue from a box nearby and dabbed her eyes and then apologized for ruining her happy moment.

"Nothing to apologize about," Erin said, brushing it off, but Kelly still felt a little stupid for crying. The thing was that's all she'd been doing for the last few weeks. She sucked in a lungful of air to gather her composure. Erin straightened and gave her a steely gaze. "Listen, why don't you come into town with us? Celebrate. We'll go out and have some drinks, a few laughs, I'm sure there's people who would be glad to see you."

Kelly gave a strained smile and drummed the table with her fingers. "Um. Sounds lovely and I am grateful but… I'm not sure I'm ready for that. People. And, not to be a killjoy but you know what they say, two's company, three's a crowd. I don't want to be the third wheel."

Erin frowned. "You wouldn't. Come on. Please."

"Thank you. But I'll pass." She pointed to her bag. "I need to finish this book."

"You mean start it?"

She cocked her head. "Same thing."

They smiled at each other. "All right, but I'm coming up here on Sunday night, okay? Just you and me. I'll bring a nice blush wine and we'll drink the night away. Sound good?" She paused and stabbed a finger at Kelly. "And I won't take no for an answer."

Kelly smiled and nodded. "Sure. Sounds good."

As Erin turned, Kelly piped up. "Oh, I forgot, my brother might be here." She grimaced. "He said he was coming up."

It didn't deter her. "Good. I finally get to meet him."

Kelly smiled.

They spent the next couple of minutes cleaning up and Kelly gave Erin a hand packing. Bryce eventually stuck his head through the hatch opening. "Ladies."

"Oh, here he is," Erin said.

"I thought I felt my ears burning." He grinned. "Kelly!"

"I hear congratulations are in order," she said as he climbed in. He glanced at Erin and Kelly could tell he was a little taken aback by the frog in her throat. Erin wrapped an arm around his waist and Bryce kissed her forehead.

"Yep, sealed the deal. Now I just need to go out and buy my ball and chain."

Erin nudged him and he burst out laughing.

"You look after her," Kelly said, wagging her finger at him.

"Oh, I intend to," Bryce replied, looking lovingly at

Erin. It had been a long time since Kelly had seen anyone look at her like that. It was hard not to feel jealous. She turned away and took some of the garbage and threw it down the chute ready to be bagged.

"By the way, Kelly. Thank you for letting us stay. And for free!" he said in a surprised manner. "I really couldn't have thought of a better place than this to propose. It's beautiful up here."

"That it is," she said looking out. The view of the sun retiring behind the western ridge in the summer months never got old. Watching the golden hues over the mountains inch back into darkness only to be replaced by a tapestry of speckled lights was something to behold. Now it was just gray, bland-looking skies.

"You are more than welcome."

He cleared his throat. "Well we should get going. Hank's getting a little antsy."

They hugged it out and Erin reminded her that she would be back in two nights. Kelly watched them disappear behind the trees before she left the wraparound deck and entered the cabin. She took some of the kindling, tossed it in the fireplace along with a couple of logs and stoked up the fire before closing the heavy iron door and peering through the glass at the glow.

"Well it's just you and me," Kelly said to Boomer who had now curled up in front of the fire. She took out her computer and placed it on the table, determined to get at least one chapter completed. The idea was all there, an outline had been brewing in the back of her mind for months, but getting it done, well that was another thing. She sat for what felt like an hour staring at a blank page, her fingers hovering over the keys, before drinking another cup of cocoa. There was no internet, and barely any cell service. Still, she had solar panels on the roof that fed down to a small charging unit which offered guests a way to juice a few small electronics just in case they wanted to try and get a bar or two. It also doubled as a way to illuminate the inside. The charging unit powered one LED lightbulb that dangled down, and could be turned on and off at the pull of a cord.

Kelly sighed. Why weren't the words coming to her? Her mind was like a highway of spaghetti, a tangled mix of the past and present. Realizing she wasn't going to get anything done, she closed the laptop, got up and filled Boomer's bowl with kibble, then grabbed a soft white towel. "Sauna time." She pointed at him. "Now don't you be getting up on the table and eating what's left of my food, okay buddy?" Boomer glanced up with these deep brown eyes of his that melted her heart. Not overly hungry, she had whipped up some pasta, and shaved off some parmesan for the top, but after a few bites, she pushed it to one side.

Kelly collected a flashlight from a drawer, snowshoes hanging off the back of the door and headed down.

The sauna was by far one of the nicest amenities at the off-the-grid rental. She'd converted an old shed into a lap of luxury so couples could pamper themselves. It was a simple setup of an all-cedar insulated interior with two benches, and an old fireplace that had been modified to contain rocks on the top. As there was no running water up to the lookout, drinkable water came in the form of two and a half gallon containers below the sink, allowing her to hand pump it in. For the bucket shower and sauna, Hank had come up with a smart way of gathering water from a nearby spring, filling up multiple barrels and then setting one high up in a tree so it could be gravity fed down to a faucet. That was then used to load up a bucket which could be poured over the rocks with a ladle to create steam.

Kelly had to use one of the fire pokers to break the ice on top of the barrel's opening to get access to the water beneath. She collected enough to fill a bucket and went into the sauna. Originally she'd opted to use candles inside the sauna but it just got too messy so she went with wall mounted tealights which offered ambiance at night. Beyond that, a shaft of daylight filtered through a small window that was two hands wide.

After getting everything set up, Kelly laid back on the cedar bench waiting for the rocks to heat up. Forty minutes later the temperature had reached around a hundred degrees before she tossed water on the rocks, and they hissed. A cloud of steam billowed and she felt her muscles relax.

She closed her eyes and perched on the edge of the bench. She breathed in deeply, letting the steam open up her lungs.

It wasn't long before she found herself thinking of that night.

Flashes of abuse tormented her mind. It was hard to forget.

It had all started with an accusation of looking too long at a male friend of Cole's. He'd had one of his work buddies over with his girlfriend for supper. They'd joined them for drinks in the outdoor hot tub. She'd always seen it as a way for Cole to flaunt and brag about arrests or new toys he'd bought. The conversation was always about him. She thought the night had gone well, until his friends left.

Nope.

The accusation was followed by a slap, and a shove, then

he grabbed her hair and dragged her back to the hot tub. Hands clamped around her throat, cutting off her air supply, he lost control and erupted, his face twisting as he struck her multiple times and then held her head under the water.

Kelly opened her eyes and glanced at the tealight set into a Himalayan salt holder beside her. Shadows danced off the walls of the sauna.

Instantly she was back there again.

Had it not been for a similar item, a heavy candle set into a metal holder beside the hot tub, she was sure he would have kept her head under the water, perhaps even killed her.

She could still remember writhing in water then grasping the steel as darkness closed in at the corners of her eyes.

What came next was swift.

Kelly struck him over the head and scrambled out of the tub, frantically running for her life.

When will the memories fade? Kelly took a deep breath and poured another ladle of water over the rocks. Her body disappeared into the cloud of steam.

Chapter 3

A cold wind howled as tree limbs scraped against a window. It was what had awoken Kelly that next morning. She tapped a button on her wristwatch. The neon glow of five forty-five shone back. It was far too early to get up. She'd planned on waking at seven, making coffee and being at her computer by eight. Nope. She squirmed beneath her duvet trying to get back to sleep but it was useless — her mind and the dog wouldn't let her. Boomer was splayed across the bed; his huge unmovable weight had her pinned to the bed, making every attempt to get comfortable impossible. She usually didn't allow him on the bed but he must have hopped up in the night. Shifting beneath him was met with resistance and a snore. "Boomer. C'mon. Move. You're crushing me," she wheezed. His gums flapped as he snored; he didn't even lift his head or blink. It was only when she scratched his back end did his tongue flop out and his body arch in euphoric bliss. The moment she stopped, he lifted his huge head and stared with groggy eyes as if to imply — *Put another dollar in the scratch machine.*

A jerk of a thumb and he got the message. Like a Slinky sliding over the edge of a staircase, he snorted and slipped forward, his front paws touching the floor before the rest followed in slow motion. "Oh that's right, just take your good ol' time. No, don't mind me." She grinned. The fire had almost gone out in the night so a thin layer of ice had formed on the windows. Even without curtains or blinds, the faint rays of sunrise wouldn't offer light for at least another hour so it was pitch dark. She'd forgotten how chilly it could get even with extra layers. Kelly pushed aside the covers, stretched and turned on the LED bulb above her. Slipping her feet into a pair of slippers, Kelly rubbed her arms as she padded over to the fireplace to throw in a few more logs. A quick stoke of the dying embers and flames soon roared to life filling the cabin with heat and a warm glow.

Kelly hand pumped water from beneath the sink into a kettle and lifted the portable butane stove onto the counter. One click later, and a bright blue flame burst to life. She set the kettle on top. Boomer scratched at the hatch. "I hear you. The call of nature is calling me too." That was the only downside to the lookout. In the summer months it was fine but when guests needed to use the bathroom in the winter they would have to don their winter gear and trudge through heaps of snow to make it to the outhouse. Kelly snagged up her jacket, boots and snowshoes and got herself ready to brave the blustery weather.

* * *

After a bright sun burst over the horizon, several hours later, Kelly was finishing up her second cup of coffee. In front of her, a cursor blinked with no text on the screen.

Ugh.

The words just weren't there. Two years earlier, her first novel, *A Call to War,* had flowed out of her like a river. Nothing could have stopped it. It really was like catching lightning in a bottle. She'd tried to think what she'd done differently. Was it the writing location? A certain drink she'd consumed? The time spent in front of the computer? The outline? She was baffled by it all. There hadn't been one day she was blocked when she wrote it, but now… now it was like someone had turned off the faucet of creativity. Nora believed she was capable of doing it again but Kelly had her doubts.

Between the constant stress of living with Cole, and the expectations of readers and the publishing world, she'd all but given up on the idea of writing another novel. Instead, she envisioned herself disappearing into seclusion like J.D. Salinger or ceasing to write for years like Harper Lee. Who would care? In her eyes she was a one-hit wonder. She imagined herself trudging around in a smelly bathrobe, muttering incoherently under her breath while driving ten feet down the driveway and back again just to collect mail.

Mail. Now that was a beast she didn't even want to think about.

After the release of *A Call to War,* she'd accumulated a mountain of fan mail almost overnight — most were from genuine folk, good people who wanted to thank her and express their appreciation, and she loved reading them... but, like any endeavor, every now and again a bad apple would make its way into the bunch. Nora said it was par for the course now that she was a bestselling author. She didn't mind but it was a little disturbing, especially at book signing events.

Her phone beside the charger lit up and vibrated. Although there was no Wi-Fi, and cellular service was spotty at best, occasionally her cell would catch a signal.

Kelly scooped it up. "Hey Mom."

"Hi darling. I thought you were going to call me when you arrived?"

"Sorry, I got busy talking to Erin and then I couldn't get a signal."

"You know I worry about you being up there."

"I know you do. Look, I'm fine. I'm trying to get started on this book and—"

"Nora called," she said cutting her off. "I gave her your number."

"I know, we spoke."

"Good. Nice lady, a bit hyper but overall nice."

Kelly smiled as she got up and refilled her cup with more hot coffee. Steam spiraled up as she poured it in, its nutty aroma awakening her senses.

"Look, I have some bad news. I just wanted to tell you that Adam won't be coming up. I'm afraid he's been called into the base. He wanted me to let you know."

She poured in milk. "You're joking? It's been two years since I've seen him and he couldn't phone to tell me himself?"

"Speak to him. I'm just passing on the message." Her mother continued. "So have you given any more thought to what we talked about?"

"Mom, I just got up here."

"I understand but…" She sighed. "I just know how busy you get with your work and a week will turn into a month and before you know it—"

"The world will end," Kelly added, chuckling. She returned to the table and cursed the blinking cursor under her breath. "Mom, I haven't forgotten. I'm thinking about it. I just need some time. Okay?"

"Are you sure you're okay? Do you need anything?"

"Mom, I'm good. If I need anything I will let you know. Besides, I can always run into town and get it myself."

Her mother grumbled. "Maybe I should come up instead."

"Mom."

"Okay. Just checking. Anyway, I'll—"

The line crackled and then went dead.

"Mom? Mom?" Kelly looked at the phone. There was no signal. "Ugh!" It wasn't the first time. In fact it was lucky if she got anything out here. Often she would hike farther up the mountain and even then getting one bar could require balancing like a gymnast and holding the phone in the air.

Kelly sighed, ran a hand over her brow and looked at

Boomer. He yawned as he rose from his lap of luxury by the fire and ambled over to the wall where his leash hung on a rusty nail. He pulled it off, returned and dropped it at her feet, then sat on his haunches staring at her. Her lip curled as she drummed the table with her fingers. "If walking you was the answer, I would have multiple books finished by now." She laughed and snatched up the leash. "All right. C'mon. Let's go." Boomer bounded around, excitement getting the better of him. "Whoa, whoa, slow your ass down."

* * *

On the ground, Kelly broke into a jog keeping Boomer at her side. She'd forgotten how much she loved to get outdoors. Running had been a way of life to her, a habit ingrained from her involvement in cross-country in high school. Even after leaving she'd continued to put in a few miles a day — making it a way of life — but like many things she'd enjoyed before marrying Cole, it was soon pushed to the back burner. His irrational distrust and need to control had stopped her from going out with friends, visiting family or doing simple things like joining a gym or running. Of course he never told her directly to stop but he didn't need to — it was all a psychological game with him, a back and forth of mood swings that put her on edge, made her sick to her stomach and daily filled her with worry.

Snow fell around her, ice crystals getting in her face. The only sound was of powdery snow crunching beneath her boots. She liked the sensation of snow, the way it sank beneath her boots and supported her at times. Unlike the treadmill she once owned, she felt like she got a better workout being in nature. It also made her mind come alive, perhaps, that would kickstart her writing.

Although overnight the earth had seen a moderate amount of snow settle. It wasn't uncommon to get up to four feet, but that morning it was nowhere close to the storm that Hank had been harping on about. There were still trail areas that weren't deep. The sky had turned a gunmetal gray and blotted out what little blue she'd seen that morning. Snow was falling fast, getting thicker and making it hard to see but that was normal for December.

They darted into the surrounding forest, slaloming around Douglas firs, pines and spruce. Boomer kept pulling hard and barking at the sight of every squirrel or rabbit.

She sucked in the crisp air, freezing the back of her throat.

Kelly basked in the natural beauty and remembered again why she'd purchased the land. Before she saw any success with writing, the lookout had been one of several rentals she wanted to develop. Ultimately she'd envisioned having a different tiny house in every state of the country and then living off the income. And, with the success of the lookout, it was beginning to look possible, that was until Cole entered the picture.

The irony was she'd been introduced to him through Erin who had cut his hair. Somehow the conversation of who he was dating came up and she'd given him Kelly's phone number, and encouraged him to call her. If she hadn't been on the search for that someone special, she might have turned down the offer of coffee, but one meeting and Kelly had to admit that the uniform sucked her in, that and his initial charm. Those early months were magical. Time together was full of kindness, gifts and frequent getaways. In fact there was nothing in the days leading up to their wedding that would have given her cause for alarm. Sure, he drank more than most, and talked negatively about some of the locals but that was expected in his line of work. He saw the worst of society. No, nothing was out of the ordinary. It was only when they tied the knot that it all went downhill.

Kelly slapped the thought of him from her mind as she slowed her pace near the edge of a rocky bluff that overlooked Stoney Lake. Nothing was moving out there, nothing but the cold. Her breathing eased, and she took out her phone, lifted it high and checked to see if she had a signal. Zero. She slipped it back into her pocket and got close to the edge, keeping a firm grip on Boomer. A few loose rocks fell, reminding her of how high it was.

In the summer months, families would come up and

picnic, accessing the lake from farther down. One year she'd caught a few teenagers who had climbed up to jump off the edge into the crystal-clear waters. She felt like an overbearing parent but she had to caution them as her property ended at the edge and she didn't want to get in trouble if anyone got hurt. Fortunately no one did. Now with winter in full swing, the surface had solidified with a layer of slick ice. She crouched and dug out a smooth stone from an exposed area of the ground and tossed it over the edge. It landed, bounced and slid across the surface. She did it again, but with force and that time it broke through. It was deceiving to look at, as some areas of the ice were thinner than others, a point that was made clear a year ago after an attempt at ice fishing turned into an emergency. The temperatures had been mild and from the little information released in the local paper, the ice gave way and two men fell in. Had it not been for a group of hunters nearby, they might have died.

Boomer growled, shifting Kelly's attention away. She looked back at him and noticed he was staring at the tree line. He tugged at his leash and she pulled him back.

"Boomer, you are not chasing the squirrels. We've already had this conversation."

It hadn't been the first time he'd wanted to take off on her. He was the type of dog that if she called out to him, he would usually return to please her rather than pursue what looked like a tasty morning snack.

Still, he wouldn't let up. "Boomer. Boomer!" she said, finding herself in a tugging match as he barked incessantly. As hard as Kelly dug her boots into the ground he was just too strong. She nearly lost her balance as the leash slipped between her gloves and Boomer shot off at lightning speed toward the tree line, his leash trailing behind him.

"Oh come on!" Kelly gave pursuit, yelling for him to come back but with her voice barely rising beyond a whisper, Boomer didn't respond. The dog disappeared into the dense forest. She groaned, red faced, with sweat trickling down her temples from jogging. "Boomer!" she cried out as she hurried to catch up.

She figured she'd find him barking up a tree. Instead, his tracks gradually got harder to follow because of how thick and fast the snow was coming down. Turning back, even her own footprints were being covered as a strong wind lifted snow and quickly created whiteout conditions. "Boomer!" Kelly yelled, her breath catching in her throat as she swallowed ice crystals.

Eventually Kelly had to lift her forearm to block the gust of driving snow. She thought she heard a bark but trying to pinpoint it in the howling gale was near impossible. It felt like she was in a snow globe with heavy flakes spinning around her making visibility almost zero. The trees loomed over, twisting and reaching down on her like gnarled fingers, each one blanketed and frozen by the harsh weather.

As soon as she wiped crystals from her frozen eyelashes more would blow in.

She continued calling for him but her dismal voice was lost.

Kelly removed her gloves and brought up two fingers.

A sharp whistle. That would do it.

Kelly let out the signal that never failed.

Nothing.

Where are you?

Pressing on through hard flakes she surveyed the terrain. There were paw prints but were they his? She couldn't be sure as there were multiple tracks heading off in different directions. Wolves? Northern Idaho had its fair share and guests had seen the odd one prowling through her property, searching for food. Some of them weighed upwards of a hundred to a hundred and thirty pounds. A shot of panic went through her. If a pack got hold of him, they'd tear him to shreds. "Boomer!" A frantic cry strained her already damaged throat. Her heart began pounding.

"Boomer!"

No response.

Kelly continued searching through the worsening weather for close to an hour without luck. It was only as she was retracing her steps did she notice a glimmer of silver sticking out of the snow. Kelly tramped over and reached down. There, buried beneath was his leash.

Surrounding it were large droplets of blood but no sign of him.

She looked up and gazed around her, a cold chill came over her.

How could this come off? The strong metal clasp required unlatching. Even if it had got caught on a limb, it wouldn't have opened. It had never opened even after he'd run off before. *No.* It required hands.

But there were no footprints, at least ones that she could see. Then again, the snow was bombarding the ground and… *Cole?*

The thought of him prickled the hairs on the back of her neck.

Backing up slowly, Kelly reached into her pocket and fished out her cell phone.

She powered it on, her eyes sweeping.

"C'mon, c'mon!" she said holding it high, trying to get a signal. Nothing. Not even one bar. She shivered, though it wasn't the cold but the grip of anxiety. She called out to Boomer one final time but it was useless, her voice, the wind, the snow, it was all working against her. She didn't want to turn back but after an hour, after finding this, she had no choice but to return to the lookout.

She jogged back with a new sense of fear.

Could he have taken him?

He'd always hated that dog.

Did he know she was back? No. That was impossible. She hadn't told anyone besides Erin and Hank. Then again someone could have spotted her at the gas station.

* * *

Not wasting any time, Kelly collected the keys to the snowmobile, ran to the shelter close to the sauna and pulled back a heavy tarp. Every sound, every movement had her senses on high alert. The engine growled to life and the machine lurched forward, tearing up snow as she took off heading for the Emery Police Department.

Chapter 4

Twenty-five minutes. That's all it took to reach Emery by snowmobile. Kelly glanced at her wristwatch, she was almost there when the weather worsened. As she burst out of the dense forest she felt the full onslaught. The initial blast of the blizzard nearly flung her clean off the machine. She tightened her grip and ducked low barreling forward through a tunnel of snow.

Even with the bright halogen headlight it was still hard to see. The gray of day had been replaced by a wall of white, blotting out trees, vehicles, and turning buildings into mounds of powder. A harsh wind howled as nature unleashed its fury and threatened to stop her.

Kelly leaned into the storm.

Am I being irrational?

It was a catch-22. On one hand Kelly knew the police could alert Cole to her whereabouts as some of his colleagues had taken his side, but on the other hand, if she did nothing and she was right, her worst fear could be realized and no one would know a damn thing until they found her remains — *if* they found her at all.

Admittingly, it was possible that Boomer's disappearance had nothing to do with Cole and that this was just her fear playing tricks on her mind, but the latch, the blood, that couldn't just happen without someone involved. On the short journey in, she sifted through every scenario of how the latch on the leash could have come off but nothing added up. The few times Boomer had got away from her in the past, he'd always returned with the leash trailing behind him.

A sharp gust of wind stole her breath, making it hard to think.

Kelly swerved onto Main Street and was coming up on the police station when she saw a police SUV parked outside the Coffee Vault. The lot was packed with locals taking shelter from the brutal weather. Kelly hunched over, squinting through the deluge of snow that swirled like a tornado. She slowed, veering into the lot, coming to an abrupt stop beside a 4 x 4 black truck. Taking a second to calm her beating heart, she killed the engine and removed her gloves, lifted the goggles but kept her hood up and scarf on. The fewer that knew she was back, the better.

Keeping her head low, she shouldered into the café.

A bell above the door rang out, a few heads noting the change in temperature. They turned away, disinterested. The aroma of dark roasted coffee beans and pastries made her stomach grumble. The Coffee Vault was a cozy little abode that could have easily gone head to head with any of the finest coffee chains. It was new to Emery; the owner was a stylish young guy with a head full of dreams and cash to burn. Patrons lined the wooden stools at the counter, packed into plush leather seating, chatted and basked in the glow of a roaring fireplace. A couple gazed up at flat-screen TVs which played current news.

Kelly stamped her boots, shook off a shell of snow and made a beeline for Officer Hurst. Kelly knew him as Lucas, a thirty-year veteran of the department, one of the good ones, the guys who weren't easily swayed by department politics or other cops looking to abuse power. Six feet of brawn, with a slightly larger than average frame, he took up two seats. He was sitting alone in a booth at the far end, most cops did. It let him keep a close eye on the door, gave a way to see who was coming, at least that's what Cole said the academy taught him. Hurst though was a different breed; he didn't seem to care who approached.

When Kelly reached the booth, he looked up over his spectacles. In front of him were a newspaper, a cup of coffee and a half-eaten apple pastry. He squinted for a second as she slipped in across the table from him without removing her hood.

His brow furrowed. "Kelly?"

She glanced to her left, hoping no one heard.

Cups clinked, a waitress carried an order, and a teenager looked up from his phone. People were too busy yakking, or drinking coffee to notice. "Lucas."

The moment he heard her croaky low voice, his

demeanor changed.

"When did you return?"

"Yesterday."

"I thought you were staying with family," he said. He wiped sugar from the corner of his mouth with a napkin before dumping it on the table.

"Needed to winterize the lookout and close it for the season."

"Couldn't Hank have done that?"

"I have a book to write."

He nodded slowly, taking a sip of his drink. "You want a coffee?"

She shook her head, her leg bounced nervously below the table. "My dog's gone missing. Took off this morning."

He offered back a confused expression.

She dug into her pocket and removed the leash to show him. It clattered as the latch hit the table. "I found this in the woods. Someone removed it from his collar. I uh…" She took a deep breath and Lucas clued in and leaned back.

He lifted a hand. "Now, Kelly, I know what you're gonna say but…"

"He hated this dog," she shot back.

Lucas went to say something but closed his mouth and looked down at it. A brief sigh, a glance around the room and then he studied her before scratching the side of his nose. "Maybe your dog just took off after an animal."

"And removed the leash?" she asked gesturing to it.

"Could have got caught on something."

"There's blood on it."

"Could have come from another animal."

She pushed the leash in front of him. "Try pulling back the clasp."

Reluctant at first, he tested it and then gave it back.

"Look. I know you're going through a difficult time but…" He was at a loss for words. "What do you expect me to do?"

Her fingers twitched on the table, she bit down on the side of her lip. "I don't know. Go over to his place. See if my dog is there."

Lucas put a hand up to his head. The radio on his chest crackled and he lowered the volume. "You know I can't do that. Besides, I think it's highly unlikely that Cole had anything to do with it."

Kelly shook her head. "Of course."

"I saw him yesterday. He said he was heading out of town."

"Yeah, probably to my place."

"No. North. A hunting trip."

She scowled. "Bullshit. He doesn't like hunting." She stabbed the table with a finger. "He knows I'm here."

"No one knows you're here, Kelly. Hell, I didn't even know you'd returned," he said looking around. "And by the looks of it, I think you want to keep it that way. Now go home. You'll probably find your dog waiting and realize—"

"That this was all in my head? Huh? Is that what he's been telling people?"

"Kelly."

She screwed up her face. "Forget it. I shouldn't have even come here," she said slipping out of the booth. "I'm sorry." Keeping her head low she crossed to the door. Glancing briefly up at the TV, she saw that the news was covering the change in weather. A red alert ticker ran along the bottom of the screen: *Winter Storm Warning in Effect Could Bring Upwards of 50 Inches of Snow to Idaho and the West.*

Hank was right.

She braced herself for the severe cold.

As she made her way back to the snowmobile, Officer Hurst called out to her. "Kelly!" She turned and squinted as he tilted into the avalanche of snow. He took out his card and gave it to her. "Listen, if you have any further problems, that has my extension on it. I'm going to be a little busy tonight with the storm but I'll keep checking my messages."

She tapped it against her glove and looked at him.

"You know I don't get much of a signal up at the peak. Wouldn't be of much use to me. But thanks." She handed it back and got on the snowmobile. Hurst stared on as a gust of snow hit him. Before starting the engine she looked at him and said, "What he did to me. I never made it up, Lucas." Then she fired up the snowmobile and tore out of the lot.

* * *

After returning from town, Kelly surveyed the property for fresh footprints in the snow. It would have been a lie to say she wasn't scared. She called out to Boomer. Nothing. Tears welled in her eyes, frustration over the damage done to her voice. She couldn't even cry out without pain. Overwhelmed by the storm rolling in, she had no other choice but to head up to the lookout.

Once inside, she emptied kibble into Boomer's bowl then took it down and placed it under the portable shelter, hoping that if he was okay and he made his way back he would take cover there and have something to eat. Going around the side of the sauna, she scooped up the axe and chopped a few more logs, then gathered up an armful.

Back inside, Kelly forced down the hatch and bolted it shut, then snagged up a pair of binoculars and went to the window and swept from side to side. It was useless. Nothing but whiteout conditions. She couldn't see within a few feet.

The lookout shook violently as a fierce gale picked up and threatened to topple it. Kelly removed her phone and gazed at the screen. *"Great,"* she muttered under her breath. The power was low, in the red, on 3 percent. Even if there was a slim chance of getting a bar she wouldn't be able to use it for long. Kelly plugged it into the solar charging unit and hoped to God that the small, almost nonexistent amount of light they'd had over the past week before the snow hit had charged the green box enough to feed the phone some juice. She tapped it a couple of times because the tiny red light which indicated that it was connected to the solar panels didn't light up. *Loose wire?* She ran her hand around the back but the cables felt snug. *Odd.* She'd seen reviews online about the unit having sporadic issues, but she'd only had this less than a year, and this was the first time she'd seen it acting strange. She considered braving the storm to check the external cables but it wouldn't matter now — it was evening — as long as the battery inside the unit held a charge she was good to go.

She flipped on the power switch so the outlets were ready. The battery voltage indicator needle shot upward and registered in the yellow which indicated that there was a small charge stored in the unit. *Oh, wonderful. Just my luck,* she thought. Erin had almost drained the battery. With the phone plugged in, a tiny LED light switched to green to let her know it was outputting a charge. *Let's hope there's enough.* Kelly lifted a heavy mallet leaning against a kindle splitter and split some of the kindling, then packed the fireplace with logs and sat back and stared into the flickering blaze, disturbed by the day.

Chapter 5

Kelly awoke to knocking. It was loud, persistent and all-pervading. It only took a few seconds to realize it was coming from the trap door. Something — someone — was trying to get in. Her insides knotted as panic crept up in her chest.

3:18 a.m.

It was still pitch dark.

Only a few dying embers glowed in the fireplace.

She didn't dare move. Who was it? Were they aware she was here alone?

Now she wished she had a gun, any form of protection. Her eyes darted to the knife block holding six kitchen blades. She could get up but the floor would creak. They would hear her. They? Who were they? One, two? How many were out there?

Thud, thud.

The lock rattled again.

Get a grip on yourself, she muttered. It wasn't like this was the first time she'd spent a night alone. There were many times Cole was on night shift. Neither was this the first time she'd been at the lookout by herself. Now she wished Boomer was here.

Boomer. A sinking feeling in the pit of her gut, yesterday's incident came back to her like a bad dream. He was still out there, somewhere, perhaps lost in the storm or worse — dead. She would never forgive herself if he was simply lost.

Kelly clenched her jaw, her pulse pounding as courage rose inside her. She slipped into slippers and donned a thick sweater before shuffling over to the counter and removing a large six-inch knife.

Another thud, followed by two more.

"Hello?" she said.

No response.

Either the howling wind was making it hard for them to hear or her nonexistent voice was — more than likely both.

Kelly got low to the floor, inches away from the hatch, and checked the lock. *Thank God for strong deadbolts.* Security had been a troubling aspect of running the lookout. Without Wi-Fi, and little to no cellular reception, it was one of the first questions guests asked. Is there a lock? What happens if someone tries to break in? Do you get troublemakers in the area? She wasn't going to say yes. She would have never booked anyone. And, it wasn't like she could leave a gun with them, or employ a security guard. They were in the middle of nowhere. It was a remote, off-the-grid rental that appealed to hikers, romantic couples, the adventurous of society. She figured they were attracted to the inherent dangers of the wild. "You should know this is private property. You are trespassing."

Then, a husky voice filtered through.

"Please. Let me in. I'm freezing out here."

"Who are you?"

"The name's Barnes. Travis Barnes. I'm a LEO forest ranger from St. Joe National Forest."

Her plot butted up against the Idaho Panhandle National Forests which was an aggregation of three national forests: St. Joe to the west curling beneath her, Coeur D'Alene and a portion of Kaniksu to the north. It was why it was common to see campers hiking through her property unaware they were trespassing, especially if they were trying to make it to Stoney Lake. "What are you doing here?"

She could hear the shivering in his voice. "I got caught in the storm, lost my way. Look, I just need to warm up. I'll freeze to death out here." Kelly had made friends with a couple of rangers from the area due to the frequent interactions with campers. She was all too familiar with their dress code and the location of the nearest station. Reluctant to open, she continued her line of questioning.

"What station you from?"

"St. Maries," he shot back without hesitation.

"Address?"

He reeled it off.

"You're a little out of the way, aren't you?"

"We got a call for lost campers from Shadowy St. Joe Campground. A group of us were out trying to find them when the blizzard hit. I got separated from the others, couldn't discern where I was. I saw the lookout and figured I could take shelter. Didn't know anyone was here."

The wind howled like an angry woman. Kelly ground her teeth together.

"I thought the LEOs were based out of the Coeur D'Alene district."

"That's right, however, St. Maries has a few of us now."

Not everyone was familiar with the differences between park rangers, forest rangers and game wardens, and even fewer knew that not all forest rangers were law enforcement officers (LEOs) — the strong arm of the law for the U.S. Forest Service.

"Give me some names of your colleagues."

"What?"

"Names. Forest rangers from your department."

"Uh…" He reeled off three, the first two she didn't recognize but the third, Ray Harding, she knew him. "Look, I'm sorry to impose but I'm freezing. I just need to warm up." He was persistent. She didn't want trouble, or to have his death on her conscience.

A few more seconds of hesitation. "Climb back down and step out where I can see you."

"What?"

Kelly repeated the question, and heard him curse before he agreed.

Wrapping a thick winter jacket around her, and slipping into boots, she opened the door to the wraparound deck and took out a flashlight. Ice-cold needles raked her face and she gasped at the freezing temperature. The cold air blew so wild that it had reduced visibility to almost zero. Still, Kelly peered over and waited for him to emerge at the bottom. Squinting into the porridge of white she could barely see a damn thing. Eventually, twenty-five feet below, the stranger trudged out into the snow and looked up, one arm briefly covering his face. Kelly shone the 1,000-lumen beam from the Maglite down and could see the green uniform. Although she couldn't make out every detail, a few minutes of staring and contemplating his answers was enough to convince her to let him in.

Kelly reentered and pulled back the deadbolt, and lifted the hatch. She waited, still clutching the knife behind her back.

Can't be too careful, she thought.

By the time Travis made it to the top he looked like a snowman covered in white from head to toe. As he climbed over the lip, the first thing that caught her attention was his duty belt, and a gun. LEOs were the only forest rangers that carried a piece.

"Thank you," he said, shivering and shaking off snow before entering.

Up close he was clean cut, a good-looking fella, shaven, dark eyes and approximately five foot ten. He removed a black beanie to reveal a full head of brown mousy hair and a small scar at the corner of his eye. He didn't look a day over thirty-five. His cheeks were flushed red, wet, and his lean figure was shivering like mad.

"Here, let me take your coat and you take this," she said handing him a warm horse blanket to wrap around him. He took a seat on one of the small foldable stools and shivered. Kelly slammed the trap door closed and threw a few more logs into the fire to warm up the abode. She returned the knife to the block. "You're lucky you found this place," she said.

He nodded, clutching the blanket around his shoulders. "Your voice. What happened?" he asked. Kelly suddenly felt very exposed and vulnerable upon realizing the scarf that she usually kept around her neck was not on. Still, it was dark and the only light came from her flashlight and the fire which was now flickering to life and casting shadows on the inner walls.

"Um." She quickly changed the topic. "Hot chocolate?"

He stared at her and nodded, breaking a slight smile of appreciation. Kelly busied herself taking out two cups and tried to learn more about him to avoid having to answer any personal questions. "So Travis. You said you were out looking for campers?" she asked while scooping two heaps of powder into mugs.

"Uh?"

"Campers. You said you—?"

"Right. Yeah. Two fourteen-year-olds. We assumed they couldn't have got far. We spread out to cover more ground, then this storm blew in and it was just a wall of white. I couldn't tell if I was going north, south…" He chuckled. "Two years on the job and I've found myself in a lot of hair-raising situations but nothing like this."

"Don't you carry a personal locator beacon?"

"We have them but I didn't have one on me. Didn't think we would be out long. You know, most of the time folks have just stepped off the trail."

"Right." She nodded. "Radio?"

He shook his head. "Tried it. Didn't work."

"Cell phone?"

"No luck."

"Yeah, a poor signal is quite common out here. You still have them… the radio and phone, I mean?" Kelly couldn't see the typical radio attached to his duty belt.

He reached for his coat, took out a phone and showed her that it wouldn't power on. After, he pointed to his belt and then patted his chest where the mic would usually be attached. "I lost the radio in the storm. I spent more time scrambling through snow on all fours than standing." He sighed. Travis ran a hand over his face. "Ah, anyway, I don't think it matters — the grid is down."

"The what?"

"The power grid."

She nodded thoughtfully, filling the kettle with water and placing it on the butane burner to heat up. "Because of the storm," she added.

He shook his head. "That's not what caused it." He looked around.

She stared back, her brow knit together. "What do you mean? The power has gone out before. Last year for instance. It was down for almost sixteen hours."

He reached down and untied the laces in his boots. "It could very well be. I'm not saying it's not that but…" He trailed off as if he knew more but didn't want to worry her.

After a few minutes the kettle whistled that it was ready. Kelly removed it from the burner and poured hot water into the mugs. A quick stir and she handed him one. "Here you go."

Travis took it with both hands and blew steam rising from the surface. "You are a godsend." A quick sip and he looked back at Kelly who remained standing. Her eyes darted to the bed and she realized how awkward this was — there was only the one.

He cleared his throat. "So… uh… what are you doing up here?"

"I own this place."

He pointed at her. "Right, you said. Private property."

She nodded. "I rent it out. Mostly in the summer but I've been testing out the last two winters."

"Huh. Any luck?"

She shrugged. "Ah, so-so. Mostly hikers, and the odd couple mad enough to brave the cold weather." She smiled back; their faces glowed in the amber light of the fire. Travis pulled at his khaki pants which were soaked through along with portions of his shirt. She set her cup on the counter behind her. "You know what... hold on a second." She rummaged around in the drawer space below the bed and pulled out a fresh pair of pants, socks and a shirt. There was underwear but she figured the situation was already awkward enough. "You look about his size," she said handing them over.

"Your husband?" he asked.

"Ex."

He made an O shape with his mouth.

Some of Cole's clothes and hers were there from the previous summer.

Kelly cleared her throat and turned to head out onto the deck when he stopped her. "It's fine, no point you getting any colder."

She nodded then turned away. His slim silhouette reflected in the window as he peeled off the damp clothes and slipped into the dry ones.

"Sorry, I forgot to ask your name?" he said, sliding a leg into one of the jean legs and balancing on the other.

"Kelly Danvers," she muttered over her shoulder.

A few seconds later he was dressed. "Well, Kelly, I really appreciate this. I had visions of breaking in and spending the night shivering." He wrapped the blanket around him and sat down. He exhaled a sigh of relief. "If you want to sleep, don't mind me."

"No... I'm... wide awake now."

He pursed his lips and gave a nod. "How long you been running this place?"

"Quite some time."

"So this is what you do for a living?"

She picked up her drink and stood across from him, still cautious.

"Actually, no, this is a side project I started several years ago." She didn't go into detail but she might as well have as the question that followed was a common one asked by those who didn't recognize her from the jacket of her book.

He swallowed and rolled his neck around to work out tension. "Cool. So what do you do?"

There it was, the question she didn't like answering.

Really, she should have had no problem, as it wasn't like she needed to be embarrassed, but for some reason she always was. It wasn't that she wasn't grateful for what she did for a living or that she wasn't proud, but there was often a weird shift in the dynamics of a conversation once she told people she was an author. She always left off the "bestseller" part in fear of sounding pretentious. Either way, there would usually be one of two responses: "Oh that's fabulous," or their voice would drop a tone lower and they would pull a face before following up with the next question. "So… you written many books?"

Often when asked, she told them no, and left it at that. Occasionally, she would say only one — at which point they would either smirk or their brow would knit together in confusion. How could that be a living? One book? Truth be told, one book rarely made authors a living, she was in the minority, some critics said.

Neither answer sat well with her.

Usually she would change the subject or tell them the name of it. She always got a kick out of those who never heard of the title or even her for that matter, as it meant they didn't act differently toward her. For some strange reason the moment people knew who she was and the title of the book, they would act like they were in the presence of a celebrity, and that was far from how she felt. Sure, she wanted people to read her book but having her face plastered over millions of copies, being found in airports, and having hundreds show up for signings, well, that was uncomfortable. That's because it wasn't her goal when she set out to write the book. If ever... the story was like an itch that just wouldn't go away. In fact, she'd shelved the idea four times, and even dumped the first draft in the garbage can. Had it not been for her mother who had noticed, it would have likely would up in a recycling plant and history would have been rewritten.

Kelly stared at him, pondering her options.

Instead of lie, she told him outright, trying to shorten the line of questioning. "I write. I'm an author. I wrote *A Call to War*. It was an international bestseller and it's the only thing I've ever written. It affords me a comfortable lifestyle. I prefer not to discuss it… if you don't mind." The words shot out then she took a sip of her drink.

His eyes grew wide and he wagged a finger. "I thought you looked familiar."

Oh great, he was in that group. Here we go. Wait for it. When are you writing the next one? Come on. You're going to say it, she thought. *So might as well get it over and done with.*

Except he didn't. Strangely, Travis simply got up and walked over to the window, his expression changed to concern as he clutched his drink. "I hope they found those boys."

Kelly breathed a sigh of relief. For once, someone who recognized her but didn't make a big deal out of it. "I hope so too," she added. Then it dawned on her. "You wouldn't have come across a German Shepherd in your travels, would you? she asked.

He turned and shook his head. "Your dog run off?"

She sighed. "Yeah. Yesterday."

Travis lifted a hand. "Hey look, if it's any consolation, dogs have a unique way of finding their way back. They're very resilient, you know. Much more than us." He looked back out again. "And of course it does help that they have all that fur."

He returned to his seat.

"Yeah, I hope you're right." She stared at him for a few seconds, shadows dancing off his features. Even though he was a stranger, for the first time since yesterday she didn't feel so isolated, alone or even scared. "Hopefully tomorrow I should be able to get a few bars and you can call your office. I can even take you into town by snowmobile. It's about twenty-five minutes from here."

He shook his head, and sucked in air. "No, it won't work."

Puzzled she replied, "Of course it will."

He swallowed a mouthful and stared down into his cup. "Like I said. I don't think the power going down is related to this storm."

She studied him with a look of confusion. "I don't understand. If it's not the storm, what else would cause it?"

Travis raised his eyes and without missing a beat he replied, "An EMP."

Chapter 6

Kelly didn't believe it.

She couldn't. Not here. Not in America. It was too outlandish to accept as true. Before the first rays of daylight filtered through the forest, Kelly had more questions than answers. EMP? She'd never heard of such a thing. Could any American say they had? It wasn't like they taught this kind of stuff in schools. It was the gossip of conspiracy groups, the paranoid and scaremongers — wasn't it?

An electromagnetic pulse. Travis went on to describe how a high-altitude nuclear detonation, a focused EMP weapon or a solar burst from the sun could emit a pulse that could knock out the grid. Electronics plugged in would be zapped, and those that weren't could still be vulnerable to the effects of the EMP because an invisible pulse radiated outward through the air.

Travis was leaning heavily toward a bomb, spouting

recent headlines in the news that backed up a theory that America was on the verge of a war — something to do with China, Iran and Russia building super-EMP bombs for "blackout warfare," however, he also said it could just be a natural event.

Was it possible? Of course.

Probable? In this day and age anything was probable.

Still, like a good segment of society, she didn't hang on every news bite, as most of it was questionable, or at least unreliable — so if an EMP bomb was responsible for a power outage, she, like others, wouldn't have known until it was too late. It wasn't that she had no interest in what was happening around the globe but with her mind lost in storytelling, most days she was lucky if she had the capacity to stay focused on watching a movie, let alone news.

"But I used my snowmobile yesterday," she said.

"As did I. How do you think I wound up this far out… walking?" He looked back at her. "While I was looking for those boys, my machine gave up the ghost a few miles from here. It just came to a standstill. That was my first inkling of what this was. I tried to retrace my steps but snowdrifts soon covered them. And before you ask, yes, there was still gas in it. That's when I tried to get in contact with my guys but the radio wasn't working, so then I tried my cell... nothing."

When asked what kind of bomb could do this, he went on to clarify that it wasn't the kind of bomb that would cause casualties directly, so to speak, because the blast occurred high up in the atmosphere, away from people. It was the power emitted that was dangerous. Depending on its distance it could disrupt, interfere with or damage electronic equipment and in turn wreak all manner of havoc on society. Like knocking over the first domino in a line. Telltale signs were power grids going down, cars and planes losing power, computer systems acting all out of whack, and backup emergency power no longer working.

And that wasn't the worst of it.

It was one thing to lose power and have random

electronics no longer working — but people depended on transportation, phones, computers — hell, the entire world today had their nose buried in a device. With advances in technology, many companies would crumble overnight without juice. Others in society would gradually lose their minds. The connected infrastructure was critical to the day-to-day running of the world. Food was the big one. Without power, without transportation, there would be no more production from factories or deliveries. Then there was heat. Not everyone had a wood-burning stove like her and with the plummeting temperatures it was more than likely the elderly would become susceptible to hypothermia.

Kelly stared back at him. "Are you sure?"

He got up and went to the window. "You said you were from Emery, right?"

She nodded.

He pointed. "You can see the lights from here. They're not working."

"But that's on a clear night. In the summer." Outside

the weather had blotted out any object within a few feet. She sighed and perched on a seat near the table. "There must be a way to verify this. To be sure."

He shrugged. "Well there are multiple ways. If you had an outlet connected to the grid there is the three-radio method but... well... it kind of relies on you already having it set up before the power goes down."

"What do you mean?"

He returned to his seat. "It doesn't matter, Kelly. It's of no use to us now."

"Well I'm interested. I want to understand."

Travis ran a hand over his long face. "Okay, well, like you asked... how can you be sure it's not just a typical blackout caused by extreme weather versus an EMP that is either geomagnetic or nuclear? Well besides the obvious, getting no power from an outlet, your car not starting or a plane crashing into your backyard, if you have three shortwave transistor AM/FM radios, here's what you can do — tune them into your local emergency frequency, extend the antennas and plug one into an outlet, the other will run off batteries, the third will need to be placed inside a Faraday cage."

"Faraday?"

"Yeah, it's a conductive envelope, basically a shield that is used to block electromagnetic fields. Think of a box of conductive metal or metal grids where an EMP pulse would be induced into it instead of the device inside. Anyway, once you have that set up, you would check the first radio after the power goes out. If you have no trouble hearing the station, chances are it's not an EMP. Backup power will often kick in at different facilities. If it doesn't power on, then you move on to the second unit which is powered by batteries. If that works, the first radio was probably taken out by a geomagnetic EMP, or some power surge from the outlet. However, if it's just a simple blackout, you would still be able to hear the radio station as mentioned before, because many stations have backup power in place. If it's a geomagnetic EMP, the radio itself would still power on but there's a good chance the stations won't work because of the EMP or because they've shut down due to the event. Basically the difference between a nuke EMP and geomagnetic EMP is there is usually some forewarning before a geomagnetic one occurs, and some stations aware of that may have taken steps to protect their equipment. Either way, the key would be to monitor that second radio for transmissions. Depending on how long the duration of the solar storm is, it could take a day or two before transmissions begin again."

"And if the second is dead?"

"Well then you're really screwed." He let out a chuckle but she didn't laugh. He continued. "If the battery-powered one is dead, then you probably have experienced a nuke EMP. That's where the third radio comes in. As long as the Faraday's shielding doesn't have any holes, leaks or such, that radio should turn on and work. Now bear in mind, there are a lot of variables that come into play, and believe me, people argue and get all uppity about the accuracies of this, but the plain fact is most don't know. Still, the kind of EMP, duration, distance, strength, frequency of nukes, and other radio stations transmitting come into play. In fact you could be looking at a couple of hours to a couple of days before transmissions return to normal, and obviously, if you're too hasty in taking that radio out of the Faraday cage and another nuke EMP hits immediately after, well, that won't work either."

Kelly stared, shaking her head. "Why have I not heard of this before?"

"It's not exactly dinner conversation."

"But in our day and age with countries pointing fingers at each other, and tensions running high, it seems we should at least be made aware."

Travis shrugged. "There's a lot of things we should be made aware of but we aren't. Welcome to planet earth," he said before letting out a chuckle. When he saw she didn't find it funny he got serious again. "Listen, one thing is for sure, it will get dangerous out there. Maybe not in the first 24 hours but once the penny drops and society realizes power won't be restored, stores will be wiped out and the worst in people will come out." He paused. "Look, I'm not a glass half-full kind of guy, Kelly, I live my life grounded in reality but it's hard to ignore the signs. At least here you have a means of staying warm, and you can hunt. In many ways we can survive here."

"We?"

"I mean — you. Once the weather is better I will hike out of here."

"You know it's a good two-hour hike to town and that's on a good day. You could be looking at three hours or more by foot with the dump of snow we're getting."

He nodded. "That's right."

She didn't want to tell him he could stay as she didn't know him well enough and there were minimal resources, the lookout only had the bare bones, but then again, sending him on his way wouldn't exactly be kind.

Kelly looked beyond the window into the darkness.

Not by any means was she one to jump the gun, or believe the first thing told to her, especially from a stranger who showed up at her door in the middle of the night with a wild tale, but a lot of what he'd said made sense — except for one thing, she hadn't checked her phone. Kelly reached for the device still plugged into the solar charging unit and hit the power switch. Nothing. No power at all.

Travis looked at her. "I told you. I'm not making this up. Whether an electronic device is plugged in or not, the pulse could affect it." It was hard to deny but then again they hadn't had any sunshine in a while, and the snow would have covered the panels, and perhaps the battery pack didn't get enough of a charge. "I'm sorry to be the bearer of bad news, Kelly, but…" He trailed off not finishing what he was about to say, but instead looking despondent.

* * *

As the night wore on, Kelly offered him the bed because of his state. At first he declined, not wishing to impose, but from the color of his skin, and the way he was shivering, he was clearly suffering. She opted to stay awake, saying she was unable to sleep. She wasn't lying either. Her mind was doing laps, circling between what he'd told her, the awkwardness of a stranger in her midst — a male one at that — and then what could be done to survive the situation. It was in a time like this she wished she'd brought a radio to the lookout to verify his claims but Cole had convinced her that it would have taken away from the experience. Of course he never objected to the idea of solar panels for phones. But then again, he said that was more of a safety issue. With little to no cellular service, she couldn't see how it improved the situation. If an emergency arose they would still have to make contact with the outside world.

As for her?

Owning an off-the-grid rental was one thing but Kelly was no survivalist. Spending a few nights here and there at the lookout was the extent of her wilderness experience and even that wasn't exactly tough. She pumped in drinking water from gallon jugs that she brought with her, Hank hauled in the wood, and if she needed supplies she was capable of doing a quick run into town to collect them. But if the snowmobile was out of action that meant hiking and if the town was in no better shape, how would that help them?

Hank. He'd said he'd be returning today. Would the Snowcat be affected?

She looked over at Travis who appeared to be sleeping soundly. Although he'd delivered a compelling case, she couldn't help but wonder if he was mistaken. What if the snowmobile was working? What if the cell phone wasn't charging because of snow on the roof covering the panels, and what if… Her mind resisted the idea that she was victim to some out-of-control event.

I have to know.

Kelly waited until daybreak before snatching up the key to the snowmobile and donning her winter gear. She glanced at Travis and eased open the trap door, careful not to wake him. A sharp, cold wind sucked out the warmth of the cabin as she descended, closing the hatch behind her.

Instantly, her body was pulverized on all sides by the

frigid weather. She hung tightly to the ice covered steps and slowly lowered into the blustery day, trying to avoid losing her grip. One slip and she could wind up on the ground, a casualty with a broken body. That was just one of the reasons why people didn't stay over the winter months.

Ten steps later, her foot slipped and she smashed her right knee into the hard wood. A cry of agony vanished, stolen by the brutal wind. Bracing herself and holding on for dear life, she continued until her boots sank into snow. She sat on one of the lower steps and slipped into snowshoes before trudging toward the portable shelter. Boomer's bowl was now gone, hidden below several feet of snow. A familiar ache washed over her. I could have done more, I should have... she berated herself but reality was there was nothing she could have done.

It was out of her control, just like the situation Travis had described.

Wiping a thick layer of snow off the machine, Kelly inserted the key and went through the process of trying to start it.

Nothing.

Again she tried without luck.

"C'mon! Don't do this to me."

She slammed a fist against the machine in frustration.

It was just another reminder of how out of control her life felt. Trying to escape Cole, trying to flee from a life that sought to confine her and reduce her to nothing more than a woman without a voice. She refused to give up, trying again, thinking that she could will the damn thing to life. But it was pointless. It was as dead as she was. Nothing more than a shell.

"I told you. It won't start," his voice cut through the howl of wind. Kelly turned to see Travis wrapped in a blanket on the lower steps. "Come on in before you freeze to death." She didn't want to but what other choice was there? Until the snow stopped, any hope of hiking out was virtually impossible.

Stuck. Confined.

Cut off from the world, this was her worst nightmare.

Chapter 7

Instant oatmeal, some homemade bagels with cream cheese, and coffee.

She stuck to the basics that morning. Kelly had begun to make it when Travis insisted she take a seat and let him wait on her. As a guest, he said it was the least he could do after she welcomed him in. At first she was reluctant but he was persuasive. Truth be told, she wasn't comfortable having him take control or seeing a uniform draped over the counter, both reminded her of Cole. It was more than off-putting to say the least.

As they sat at the table overlooking the snow-covered forest, Travis said it was the best bagel he'd had in a long time. Whether he was just saying that to be kind or being truthful, it was hard to distinguish as Kelly was so used to being put down, real compliments seemed ingenuine.

The conversation gradually drifted toward questions of a more personal nature, like her ex-husband. He wanted to know what he did for a living, and why they separated. It was to be expected, now that Travis was wearing his clothes, but she really didn't want to get into a whole spiel about abuse, or being a victim — the last thing she needed was pity, especially if they were to be stuck inside the lookout for an unknown amount of time. So, instead she talked around it, notched it up to incompatibility, and Cole's insecurities. It wasn't a lie. After *A Call to War* became a bestseller and she began getting requests for media interviews, and traveling took precedence, Cole began acting even worse than before. Jealousy. That's what she'd concluded. *You think you're so much better than me,* he would say while giving her a disgusted look. *You think because you earn more than me, I should be grateful?*

It was all nonsense. She'd never once said or acted in a way that might make him feel inferior, and yet no matter how often she tried to make it clear that the acclaim that came with publication meant nothing, and it hadn't changed the way she felt about him, he didn't believe it. He thought she would leave, take off with someone better. How? How could that possibly happen when he'd already made her feel like he was the best she would ever get? He'd stripped away at her confidence, practically robbed her of what joy she once had. Could she have done better? Damn right she could. Should she have left him sooner? Of course, but how many women like her had waited, suffered in silence and stuck it out, hoping that things would improve, that a partner would change?

Kelly felt like such a fool, and yet she knew she wasn't alone

She could still recall that first night he struck her, and how he blamed her for what happened. Kelly looked at Travis and decided to leave out the tale of abuse from the conversation.

"Did you resent him?"

Still lost in her thoughts she snapped back into the present.

"Sorry?"

"Your husband. You said he was jealous of your success."

She frowned and swallowed hard. "Um. No. I actually understood how it could make a person feel less than, if they wanted it to, but… well… I write, he saves lives. How could anyone compare the two?" She swallowed her food. "If anyone should feel less than, it's me. At least he was leaving this planet for the better, well, before…" She stopped herself again, almost treading into uncomfortable waters. She sighed. "My novel might stand the test of time but eventually like all books, it will disappear below mounds of new bestsellers, find its way into a bargain bin at a used bookstore and become nothing more than the ramblings of a woman who at one time thought she had something to say."

"Do you?"

Her brow knit together. "Do I what?"

"Have something to say?" He said, then scooped another spoonful of oats between his lips. She breathed in deeply and contemplated the question.

"I used to think I did."

"So what changed?"

She paused and looked out the window. "Me I guess. I mean I could blame Cole, and believe me, he deserves a whole lot of blame but the reality is I stayed with him far longer than I should have and…" She breathed in deeply. "No matter how I try to justify my reasons for staying longer than I should have, that's on me."

He nodded thoughtfully.

Gradually, she was able to swing the conversation around to him. Unlike her, he seemed to have no problem discussing his love life, or lack thereof.

"So I see you're not wearing a ring. Never married?" she asked, taking a sip of coffee.

"Nope."

"Kids?"

"None."

"Dating?"

"Unfortunately no…" He smiled and tapped his spoon in the air. "Though there is someone special that's caught my attention recently."

"Really?"

He pulled a face. "Ah, time will tell. We'll see."

"Does this lady have a name?"

He grimaced. "I prefer not to say. You know… I don't want to jinx things and all."

"Well is she blond, dark-haired, tall, curvy?"

"I really don't like to place labels on women. It's so…" He stared off above her head. "Limiting, don't you think?"

His answer caught her off guard. It was a strange reply. "In what way?"

"Well, dating sites seem to have made it so sterile. You know… boiled it down to a specific number of traits, age, color, shape and so on and then we either fit into that or we don't. There's little room for what's buried beneath. The real stuff that matters. No one seems to care about that."

She cocked her head. "They do leave a section for interests."

He smiled again. "Of course they do but does anyone really pay attention to that?"

"Women do."

He pulled a face. "C'mon. I'd beg to differ."

She put her fork down. "So you think women only pick based on looks?"

"Looks. Career. What a man earns."

Her brow furrowed. "But how's that any different than what men do? They're all about looks."

"That's where you'd be wrong."

She chuckled. "Please. You expect me to believe a guy doesn't place priority on the way a woman looks over everything else?"

"Not every man's like that."

"So you're interested in what? Her hobbies? Her social life?"

Travis tapped the side of his head. "The mind. There's a lot more to be found inside there," he said. "Besides, eventually looks fade, hobbies and interests change but the stuff that's up in there, that's where the real gold is to be found. Unfortunately not many people open up and show that side of them, you know — the deeper parts, the light, the darkness, what really makes them tick, and who they are when no one is looking."

Kelly was intrigued by his response. Though she wasn't sure if he was pulling her leg or being serious. She sat back and breathed in deeply. "Give me an example."

He gestured to her. "You for instance. Would I be wrong to say the image you portray isn't who you really are?"

"That depends."

"On?"

"Who you ask. Ask my mother you'll get one answer, ask my agent, you'll get another."

"Ask a fan?" he asked.

She stared back at him. "I can't share my whole life with fans."

"But you already have, have you not? Don't all authors put some of themselves into their work?"

"Sure. Or maybe they're just exploring a segment of society that intrigues them, shining a light on it and giving their perspective. Not really saying it's them but how they perceive it."

He nodded slowly. "It still reveals a lot about who they are. Don't you agree?"

She smiled. "I think if we journey down that rabbit hole, we may never come back." She chuckled as she shifted the conversation away to anything that didn't involve her book or her personal life.

They continued to talk for several hours, until they had drained a pot of coffee. Then they began to clean up. Earlier she'd hung his uniform over a line that was slung between two hooks. While checking for damp spots, she noticed the nametag was missing. It seemed odd being as it was a metal pin. The chances of losing it were slim. "Huh. You know you're missing your nametag."

"It's not missing. I forgot to put it on. And trust me, it's not the first time I've forgot. I don't do it on purpose. It's just when I throw it in the wash, and then I'm in a hurry the next day, it happens. Oh you should hear my boss, he gives me heck about it all the time. Unprofessional," he said forming quotes in the air.

"Oh." She nodded. "Well the rest of your clothes are nearly dry."

"Hey look, Kelly, I really appreciate all you're doing."

She gave a thin smile. "No problem."

As Kelly was straightening his clothes, something he said in the early hours of the morning came to mind. It caught her as unusual and although she didn't want to make the situation awkward at the time, Kelly had to ask now. "Earlier you said you could see the town from here."

"No, I said you might be able to see the town's lights."

"Uh. No, you said you could, which implies you have seen the lights from up here before. And since it's winter, it wasn't when you came up. How would you know that?"

He stopped washing dishes and gave her a puzzled expression. "I mean we're at a high elevation, right? It seems to me you would be able to see it."

She narrowed her gaze. "Would, could, they are two different things." She squinted at him and then looked back at his uniform. "Something doesn't add up here."

Before she could say anything more he interjected.

"All right, all right, I didn't want to tell you but… I've been here before."

"What?"

He took a dish cloth and wiped his hands, then tossed it over his shoulder all nonchalant like he was conveying something she already knew. "As a guest. I stayed here, last year. That's how I knew about the place. I figured it would be empty."

She looked at him with a confused expression.

"Why wouldn't you tell me that?"

"Because I could tell you were nervous. I didn't want to put you on edge any more than you were," he swallowed hard, "… are, I mean."

"When were you here?"

"Last year."

"No. Month, week… day?"

Travis shrugged. "I can't remember the exact date. It was like mid-July. It was a weekend."

She was away on vacation in July, a couples retreat,

Cole's idea to try and work on their marriage. What a joke that was. Erin had been handling all the bookings at that time. There wasn't a lot to collect: name, number, payment was all handled by a third-party company that she'd partnered with to make her life easy. They forwarded the funds to her bank. Any personal details collected were basic.

Kelly crossed the small space to a drawer just to the right of him and pulled out a folder and flipped it open. She thumbed through pages until she reached July of last year. Her finger slid down one page, then the next.

"Why I am not seeing you in here?"

"What is that?" he asked leaning in.

"A guestbook. I ask that everyone sign and leave a comment. It gives me a way to see what people liked or what I can improve later." She tapped the paper with her index finger. "There is no Travis Barnes in here." Kelly turned to face him, suddenly feeling very vulnerable again, the same way she had when she let him in, the same way she did before Cole hit her.

He got a serious look. "That's because I never signed it."

"Well that's obvious, the question I'm asking is why? And don't lie to me. Cause I will find out. A friend of mine who handled the booking at that time is coming up today, and believe me, in her line of work, she has a knack for remembering names."

He shrugged. "Listen, I never saw this book, and I wasn't told to fill it out. So, I'm sorry if that changes things or makes you feel any less trusting of me but the rest is true. I was here. And that's how I know about seeing Emery."

She eyeballed him to gauge if he was lying. Under most conditions she would have told him to leave but she was stranded in the middle of the woods, hours from civilization and if anything happened no one would know. If she attempted to run... where could she go? The snow was too deep, it would be like trying to run through waist-deep water.

There had been a few instances of people not signing,

though that wasn't for a lack of them knowing, they just chose not to. She stood there for a few seconds unsure of what to say. The atmosphere was even more awkward. "Okay," she said not wishing to make waves.

He raised an eyebrow. "We good?"

"Yeah, I guess."

"You sure?"

"It's fine," she said closing the folder and sliding it back into the drawer.

"Look, maybe you can tell me about your book or what you've been working on. I gather you must be working on something, right?"

She waved him off. Her mind was like a minefield. "That's the last thing I want to do."

"But I'm interested and we don't have TV or internet to entertain us… but I did eye a copy of your book." He crossed to the bed and reached beneath the countertop where there was a library of classic novels, magazines and non-fiction related to outdoor living. *A Call to War* was among them, and it was definitely not one she'd put there.

"What the...? I never put that there," she said, as he showed her.

Travis shrugged. "Well someone did, and... while I know you don't seem too keen on having people know you wrote it... but uh... your face is on the back," he said turning it around. "Kind of hard to mistake you, unless you changed your hair or..."

"Had plastic surgery," she said as they both laughed. "That's what I told my agent." Her chuckle faded as she took the book from him and her eyebrow rose. "You didn't put this here, did you?"

"I would love to take credit for that but, sadly, no."

She wasn't sure whether to believe him. "Good." She glossed over the front cover one more time and put it back between one of Jack Kerouac's novels and *The Big Burn*. The truth was it wasn't the book, or the response from fans that bothered her, it was its connection to the first time Cole had hit her. The night she received news of hitting the bestseller list. It was meant to be a night of celebration, instead it ended up with her on the end of his fist. The only way he could bring her down was to attach himself to its publication, to justify his reaction by reducing her to his level and making her regret writing it. She hadn't told anyone that.

"Hey, c'mon now," he said taking it back out. "I told you about the EMP because you were interested… fair's fair…" His lip curled. "I'm interested in this."

She frowned, hoping he would change his mind. "Really?"

"How often does someone wind up in a remote fire lookout with a bestselling author — and the book to boot? Please." He pointed to a chair and then took a seat across from her. "Just a few words. I've always loved a good story."

Kelly grumbled under her breath as she took a seat, opened the book and looked at the first chapter. It had been years since she'd written those words, years since its publication, and a long time since she'd done a public reading. Even as she began to read the first line, it felt strange. Though the words were familiar, they reflected a very different place and time in her life, and that was both exhilarating and scary.

Chapter 8

Pick your moment. Act too soon and you stand the chance of winding up in the ER. Act too late and the ER might not even be able to help. It's the one thing every person learned from an abusive relationship. Man. Woman. It didn't matter.

Kelly didn't trust him. She wasn't a fool. All the red flags were there. There were no two ways about it. Lie once, and there was a damn good chance he would do it again, the question was why? In a relationship people lied for many reasons, to avoid an argument, to avoid petty retribution, or in her case, to avoid a backhand, but a stranger — what reason could he have to withhold the truth?

No, play it safe, Kelly. Don't rock the boat. Go along with it for now.

Wait for the right time to make your move.

That afternoon, Travis hunched in front of *A Call to*

War, sipping on hot tea as she prepared lunch. As she folded foil over a pile of meat, veggies and potatoes to cook inside the fireplace, she eyed the gun on Travis' duty belt that hung over the corner of the headboard. It was hard to ignore — an ever-present threat or opportunity. Earlier she'd gone through a variety of scenarios, ways she could escape, and yet some part of her couldn't help but wonder if she was blowing things out of proportion. Was there truth to what he'd told her? If he had wanted to hurt her he'd already had plenty of opportunity, and if he'd wanted to rob the place, again, he would have done it by now, which made her second-guess and question if her fears were rational. Okay, so he'd withheld information about being here before, and he hadn't signed a guestbook, and his nametag wasn't on his shirt... but he'd been right about the snowmobile not working and the cell phones not operating, perhaps her instincts to protect herself after years of living under Cole's thumb had made her more wary than she needed to be.

Still, she couldn't shake the feeling that something

wasn't right. Manipulation was a key component in any power struggle. She'd experienced first-hand how twisted and clever a person could be. Kelly remembered the way Cole would turn arguments around on her and make it seem as if she was the mentally unstable one. He had this knack of making her question whether she was at fault, that maybe she'd brought it upon herself, and that his lashing out was a natural consequence of a man driven to his breaking point.

It wasn't like he was prone to violent outbursts. His position as a police officer forced him to be in control, to remain calm and composed in stressful situations. That's why close friends had a hard time believing her — in the eyes of those who knew him, he was kind, caring and very much in control of his emotions.

She knew otherwise.

"Hey, um, we're running low on logs. Would you mind going down and bringing some up?" Kelly asked. "Then I'll get this lunch on."

Travis looked up from the book. "Sure. You know,

Kelly, you've written one hell of a novel. And I say that from someone who is very picky about reading material." He dog-eared a page and set it down before reaching for his Forest Service coat.

"Oh you know, that's not dry yet. But you can use this one," she said taking a thick jacket that belonged to Cole off a hook near the doorway to the deck.

Travis smirked as he shrugged into it. "I know what you're doing, Kelly."

Her stomach dropped. *Remain calm.* She gave him a puzzled look. "And that's what?" Her stomach twisted, a feeling that he was on to her. Had she stared too long at the gun?

"You're fatting me up for the kill, so to speak," he said. "Like the wildlife out there."

"Ha," she replied chuckling and pointing at herself. "You got me."

As he lifted the hatch and climbed out, he continued. "I saw you had a bottle of red wine on the counter, maybe we can have a glass with lunch, what do you say?"

"I'd say I know what you're doing, Travis Barnes."

He chuckled. "And what would that be?"

Her eyes flashed. "Taking advantage of an isolated woman. Getting her drunk."

Travis couldn't hold in his amusement. "Dang, and I thought my plan was airtight," he said in jest as he disappeared down the ladder, closing the door behind him. As soon as he was out of sight, Kelly's smile faded. She waited a minute or two until she couldn't hear him on the stairs before she rushed to his duty belt and took out the gun. The magazine chamber was empty. She rifled through the mag pockets but they were gone too. What the heck? Setting the gun on the counter, she bit down on her lower lip gently, thinking for a second. Then, without wasting another moment, she fished into his pocket for his cell phone.

Once she had it, she tapped the button on the front but nothing happened. She turned it over and checked the edges looking for a power button. Convinced he would return soon, she got up and went over to the window. Travis was loading several logs into his arms while a heavy snow blasted him.

Flash. The screen blinked on.

Kelly looked down in surprise.

While looking out she'd been holding down the button on the edge, fully expecting nothing to happen, but then the screen came alive with the manufacturer's logo. *What the heck? This shouldn't be working. He said it wasn't working.* It took less than two seconds for it to load. Before her was a lock screen and the wallpaper was set to an image of a middle-aged woman with short blond hair, attractive, with her arms wrapped around two children who couldn't have been more than ten years of age. Kelly noticed a wedding band on the woman's ring finger.

You said you weren't married, and you didn't have kids, she thought.

Another lie?

Her mind began racing.

If his phone was working, was hers?

The sound of boots on the staircase far below caught her attention.

Quickly, Kelly tucked his phone back into his coat pocket and went over to where her phone was plugged into the solar charging unit. She fumbled with the power button but got nothing. Had there been less power in the battery than she thought? She recalled it being in the yellow when she'd plugged it in. Had he unplugged the cable? The light on the unit wasn't on. His footsteps were getting louder. She was about to check the cable at the back of the panel to see if it was loose but that meant pulling it out and there wasn't time for that. That's when she noticed the cable that went to her phone was loose. It was in, but wasn't fully connected. She could have sworn she'd checked that.

Click. She pressed it back in.

Thud. Thud. Thud.

His boots pounded the steps.

Any second now that trap door would rise.

She backed away from the solar charging panel and

returned to the lunch she was preparing. No sooner had she placed her hands on the foil than she noticed out the corner of her eye his gun, still out of its holster, set on the counter.

Shit. She reached for it just as the trap door opened.

"Whoa," Travis said. "Don't shoot."

She chuckled, holding it away from him. "Well that would rely on it being loaded." She flashed the empty butt end of the gun. "It helps to have magazines — if you want to protect yourself," Kelly added, acting all calm and collected as he climbed inside and dumped the logs where the others were beneath the counter. She returned the gun to its holster. "I hope you don't mind, my ex used to carry a Glock. I was interested in seeing what forest rangers were packing."

He gestured to the gear. "Pretty much the same. Glock, two mags, ASP baton, OC, cuffs, radio, taser and a flashlight."

She tapped his duty belt. "It appears, though, you're missing the most important equipment. But I expect you forgot to include them in your kit, like your pin, right?" Her eyes narrowed. It felt like a chess game and she had sandwiched him on all sides.

Travis leaned against the counter, wiping snow from his forehead, studying her. "Nothing gets by you, does it?" He took a few steps toward her and she felt her insides tighten. He stopped inches away, then brushed past and reached into his jacket. He proceeded to remove three empty magazines.

Too focused on the pocket he'd placed the cellular phone in, she didn't check the other. "The international emergency sign for distress is three of anything: three shots, three blasts on a whistle, three flashes of a mirror, or three fires evenly spaced apart. When I got lost I fired off what rounds I had in the hope that one of my colleagues would hear me. With hypothermia setting in, I got a little desperate, you might say. I blew through what ammo I had. Does that answer your question?" He handed the magazines to her with a deadpan expression and turned and sloughed off his winter gear. He had this wry smirk on his face. If he was lying, he was good, but would he have an answer for the married woman and two kids displayed on the lock screen? Kelly looked down at the cold metal magazines in her hand. Yeah, of course he would, he'd just say it was his sister and nephews. But... one thing he couldn't answer was why his phone had power, unless there wasn't an EMP, and he was mistaken, in which case, why then was her snowmobile not working? Why hadn't her phone charged? And why had he lied about his phone not powering on?

After removing his jacket and hanging it on the back of the door, Travis fished through a drawer and removed a corkscrew, then looked at her. "I assume you want a few of these logs in the fireplace... that is if you plan on us having lunch?"

Kelly snapped out of it. "Yeah. Right. Um." She returned the empty magazines to his duty belt. While he was adding wood to the fire, and stoking up the flames, she went back to what she was doing.

Gradually, as the afternoon's light waned and they

drifted into early evening, Travis leaned back. His dark eyes looked sleepy. He also looked less bothered by the day's events, though it probably helped that he'd consumed several glasses of wine. He even told her not to worry after she apologized for her line of questions which implied that he wasn't being truthful, something she still wasn't convinced about.

In fact, there was one thing she still wanted to check, just to be safe.

"You think you can give me a hand unloading the snow from the panels?" She pointed to the large flaps of red plywood that stuck out above the windows, covered with a layer of corrugated steel to protect the wood. There were eight, two for each side of the fire lookout, and each one was propped up by two posts. In some of the old fire lookouts, the panels were hinged to fold down over the windows to prevent anyone from breaking in. They were usually closed in the winter months. Kelly was used to leaving them up as they rarely got this kind of snow but now she had no choice. "If I don't do it now, those posts are liable to give way from the weight. That's the only downside to getting such a large dumping of snow."

"Yeah, no problem." He took a swallow of wine and got up. He widened and closed his jaw, rubbing it as if he was working out a kink. His eyebrows rose as he steadied himself against the counter. "Wow, that wine's pretty strong."

"Yeah, it has a way of creeping up on you," she said slipping into her boots. Kelly had purposely only drunk half a glass as she wanted all her faculties to remain razor sharp. After donning a hooded jacket, gloves and a thick scarf, she looked at him. "You ready?"

He gave a nod and she swung open the door that led out to the deck which was now covered in a foot of snow. Keeping her head low, she forged to the left, a gust of wind battering her and taking her breath. Kelly gestured for him to handle the opposite side while she did the other two nearest to her. "Be careful when you knock out the posts as the weight of the snow will force the panel down and is liable to slam you into the window.

Happened to me last year."

Travis gave a thumbs-up.

The reason she wanted him away from her was the solar panels and wiring that came down into the charging panel was on her side and it was the only thing she hadn't checked. Working on the first panel, he peered through the window at her and watched as she took out the posts and slowly lowered the panel until a huge wedge of snow slid off to the ground. She made sure he was doing it right before moving on to the next. When she made it to where the cables ran out of the cabin and up to the roof, Kelly lowered a panel and dropped down to check if they were in.

They weren't.

They had been completely removed.

Had they been slightly loose she might have thought the wind had done it but the cables didn't come out easily, especially in the winter.

She knew they were working prior to her run.

Kelly jammed the cable back in, then continued on,

though she took a moment to get up onto the railing and clear off the snow from the solar panels. Not that it would help as it had been overcast since the blizzard had started, but it gave her a chance to check if the panels had been tampered with. Nope. They looked fine.

As she lowered herself and went to see how he was doing, she turned right into him. "Oh, I didn't see you there."

He gave a menacing expression. "Be careful getting up there, you don't want to slip. It's a long way down," he said. Had he seen her plug the cable back in? Was he growing tired of her questions?

"Yeah, thanks. All done."

She gestured for him to head in, preventing him from knowing that she'd plugged the cables back in. It was clear someone had tampered with them to prevent the phone from charging — and it was hard to imagine it was anyone else but him — but why?

It still made no sense.

As soon as they entered, Travis turned to remove his

jacket. Kelly noticed the charging light which indicated the solar panel was connected was glowing. It was the same light that indicated the battery pack had juice. Thinking fast, she threw back her hood, removed her beanie and tossed it to cover the unit.

"Hot drink?" she asked, hoping to distract him.

Chapter 9

Kelly's heart was pounding, the tiny hairs on the back of her neck were erect. At any moment her phone would flash on to show it had enough charge. It did it every time. Whether at 100 percent or not, the screen would light up indicating it was ready to use. What then? The gig would be up. He'd have to explain why her phone was working.

Three hours had passed without incident. Outside the blizzard had eased but snow was still falling heavily. After a simple meal of grilled cheese, they'd spent the early part of the evening discussing her book over a game of checkers. His fascination with her writing only intensified. At first it was to be expected but then it bordered upon uncomfortable. She'd tried to turn the tables, get him to open up about his life, where he lived, who his friends were, in an attempt to learn more, perhaps even catch him in another lie, but he kept his cards close to his chest and swung the conversation back to *A Call to War*. Travis questioned her motivations, probed for answers she couldn't give and wanted the skinny on how her writing tours, book signings and interactions with fans were conducted before he raised the question of the next book.

"So you came here to write?" he asked, running his finger around the top of his cup.

"Attempt. Though lately, I haven't been in the mindset to do anything."

"Huh. Now I feel as if I'm infringing upon your creative space." He rose from the table. "Please. Don't let me stop you."

She waved him off with a chuckle.

He gestured to the table. "No seriously, I would love to watch the magic happen."

Kelly chuckled. "Believe me, there is no magic. It's caffeine fueled, mind numbing, grunt work that some days is easy but more often than not, it's just a whole lot of staring at a blank page, watching a cursor blink."

He shifted from one foot to the next. "You make it sound like torture."

"Believe me, at times when a deadline is looming and the words don't flow it can feel that way." She rose from her chair and tossed the final dregs of hot chocolate down the sink and pumped the faucet to wash it away. "Don't get me wrong. It's a very rewarding career, and I'm fortunate to be in the position I am." She sighed. "I couldn't imagine doing anything else but… like anything, it has its moments. At least, lately."

As he approached the sink, Travis set his cup down. "I was thinking about the sleeping arrangements."

Her mind was so preoccupied by the strangeness of the situation and worrying about what would happen when her phone came to life that Kelly hadn't given it a passing thought.

She gestured to it. "You can have the bed."

"No, you're too kind, Kelly. I'm a guest, and an infringing one at that, however, what we could do since we are in this together is you could sleep under the blankets on one side, and I'll sleep on the top on the other."

Was he joking?

Before she could reply, her phone let out that familiar chime, and a burst of dull light emerged from beneath her beanie. The glow pierced the wool. Both their eyes bounced to the charging panel. She looked back at him for a second to gauge his reaction before Kelly darted across the room and scooped it up.

"Power?" she said, showing him the phone, her brow furrowing. There were multiple text message notifications.

"I can explain."

She lifted a hand. "No need. It seems things are okay."

"Kelly, just hold on a second."

"For what? I'm heading into town."

As she shrugged into her jacket and boots, he tried to get her to reconsider.

"The snowmobile isn't working."

"Really?? Like this wasn't?" she said lifting her phone.

She turned and headed for the hatch, he darted in front of her with his hands out. "Wait."

"For what? Move out of the way, Travis."

"I can't do that. You're not safe out there. We need to stay together."

Her brow furrowed. "The grid is not down. There is no EMP. You were wrong, now step aside." Still clutching the phone she tried to get by him but he prevented her.

"I can't do that."

Kelly took a few steps back and slid the phone into her pocket. "What is this?"

She studied his face.

"I told you. It's an EMP."

"Bullshit. Why did you lie to me?"

"I didn't."

"No? Then why did your phone power on?"

His eyes darted to his forestry jacket. Kelly continued, "I saw that married woman, those kids. Let me guess, not yours?"

He lifted a hand. "Look, I know how this might look but I can explain." He pointed to the table. "How about we take a seat, have a drink and…"

She pressed forward. "Screw the drink. Move out of the way."

He refused to budge and stood firm over the hatch. "You don't understand. The grid is down," he said in a strong tone.

"The phone had one bar."

"Backup power. I told you, it…"

"Enough! You unplugged the cable to the solar panels and loosened the cable to the battery pack. Didn't you?"

When he didn't answer fast enough she took that as a yes and darted for the door that led to the deck in the hope that he would move — sure enough, he moved from the hatch and she went for it. Travis crashed into her, knocking her back against the sink and causing her to cry out in agony.

"Look, I don't want to hurt you but…"

Before he could finish, she grasped the pot of hot

chocolate she'd boiled on the butane stove and tossed it at him. While it wasn't at boiling point it was still hot enough to burn, however, at the last second he raised an arm preventing the splash from striking him directly in the face. Angered, he threw her down on the bed and she hit her head on the corner of the headboard, sending a jolt of pain through her skull. "Now look at what you've made me do."

Travis clambered on top as Kelly kicked and thrashed. Twisting over, she latched on to the OC in his duty belt. All the while he was trying to control her like a wild animal. "Stop fighting me. I don't want to hurt you but you're starting to piss me off." As he flipped her onto her back, she squeezed off the OC. A thick orange spray erupted, shooting into his eyes and mouth. Travis released his grip, bringing his hands to his face as he gasped for air, and tried to stop the pepper spray from burning his eyes.

Even Kelly started coughing.

Temporary blindness, a swift kick to the nuts and Travis doubled over in agony.

In an instant, Kelly was up, and scrambling. She quickly unlocked the hatch and lowered herself down and out. The desire to get away from him was so strong that she was willing to hike out if need be. A blast of arctic temperatures and she sucked in the cold air. The steps were steep, the speed of her descent, dizzying. By the time Kelly made it to the bottom, she could hear Travis screaming at her, cursing loudly. The wind roared in her ears as she plunged into waist-deep snow. In her haste to escape she'd forgotten to grab snowshoes; now she was struggling, tripping, flailing like a fish out of water. Every few seconds Kelly cast a glance over her shoulder to see if he was on her tail. Snowdrifts blew hard into her face, threatening to wipe her out at any second. The terrain blurred before her as the force of Mother Nature battered and swallowed her in a wall of white.

Where the hell is the shelter?

She squinted. So thick and heavy was the blanket of snow that everything looked alike. Working off memory she forged ahead. All she could do was press on, tramping and struggling to make it to the snowmobile.

If her phone was working, it had to be something else.

It had worked on the day she went into town.

He must have tampered with it.

Unable to see more than a few feet ahead, she kept her hands out until she made it, breathless, her lungs seared by pain. Kelly brushed off snow and lifted the hood, took out her phone and shone the flashlight over the engine. Almost immediately she saw it. Reaching in she pulled up what remained of a wire that had been cut. With a stab of terror, Kelly twisted at the cry of Travis. "Kelly!"

She tucked the phone into her jacket.

Peering into a wall of white she knew she was hours away from civilization. There was nothing out there, no house, no road, no ranger station in miles. Trudging into the woods in these wintry conditions would have been pure suicide. Without snowshoes she wouldn't make it far. And with evening upon her and no idea where she was going, she wouldn't make it twenty yards let alone survive two hours. They'd probably find her body, buried, frozen, weeks later.

Behind her, Travis was hurrying to close the gap. "Kelly!" he shouted. His flashlight beam cut into the darkness revealing a curtain of snow.

Blinking ice crystals out of her eyes, she knew her choice was limited. She turned on the jets, propelled by pure fear and desperation. Like wading through thick mud she struggled toward the closest structure — the sauna.

At least there she could lock the door, stay warm and hopefully get a signal.

Kelly powered away from him, making the best of what little sight she had. Her legs plunged deep into snow, bobbing and stumbling forward, using her arms like paddles. Her vision was so poor that the structure only came into view when it was a few feet away. Her feet stumbled over the platform's steps.

Another angry shout. Nearer this time.

Fear gripped her.

Only one thought pushed through her mind: Escape.

As she slammed into the wall of the sauna, her lungs were on fire. It took every ounce of effort to pull the door open as several feet of snow was preventing it from moving. "C'mon!" she shrieked, looking over her shoulder as Travis got closer.

She never did get it completely wide.

Kelly managed to open it just enough to squeeze through the tight gap.

She slammed the door and drove the lock home just as Travis appeared on the other side. Through the small but thick glass window he glared at her. His skin was flushed, red, burnt from the OC spray, his expression a picture of fury.

The door rattled as he shook the handle violently from the other side.

"Open up!" He bared his teeth like a wild animal.

Travis continued to pull on the handle, convinced he would get in, but she'd built it well, with strong, thick walls to contain the heat of the sauna. However, the noise of shaking reverberated around the small space, making her think the walls might collapse. "Open up!"

"Who are you? Why are you doing this?"

His expression changed from anger and a smile flickered. "Oh c'mon, Kelly. Stop playing games. I was willing to go along with it for a while but now I'm just getting tired. After all this time? Think! If anyone should know, it's you."

She took a few steps back. No, this wasn't happening to her.

Kelly wracked her brain. Who was he? She went through the Rolodex of her mind, thinking of every interaction she'd had with locals, ex-boyfriends and even friends of Cole. She couldn't place the face. He was a complete stranger.

Travis continued to pound on the door, even stepping back and kicking it. Her heart leaped in her chest as she held the handle to ensure it wouldn't open. While she was confident the lock would hold, there was no telling if he could break in. The only saving grace was all the deep snow that had fallen made it impossible to charge the door.

Tears welled in her eyes, her throat stung. She reached up and blood trickled down the side of her face. Kelly slumped behind the door.

She stared absently around at all the wood paneling, and the stove for heating rocks. A pile of wood was below it and a firestarter hung on a hook. "Just open the door, Kelly. I don't want to hurt you."

Minutes passed. Her back jolted forward as he kicked the door multiple times. She thought he would never stop. Then, the muted sound of a phone ringing. It was low, almost indistinguishable. It was her ringtone. She fished a hand into her jacket pocket only to feel nothing. *No. No. No.* Her hand went into the other side and came out empty. But if it wasn't in her pocket, where was it? She turned and pressed her ear against the door, that's when she could hear it clearer. Rising from the floor she peered out the double-paned glass and saw Travis bending over, reaching into the snow. *No, no, no!* He straightened and in his hand was her phone. A smile formed as he returned and pressed the phone against the glass showing her the caller ID.

Erin.

There before her was Erin's face, her full name and number.

"Erin Miller. Friend? Guest?" he asked. "C'mon, Kelly. Time to come out. You can't stay in there."

Please. Please. Let it be her calling to say she can't make it. That something had come up or that the roads were too bad.

Kelly backed away from the window and that only frustrated him even more. He returned to banging on the door, rattling the handle and revealing a whole new level of crazy. They stared at one another through the thick frosted window. His eyes boring into her, his features twisting in horror reminded her of that night, the moment when Cole almost killed her.

Thud, thud, thud.

In an instant, Travis ducked out of view and vanished, disappearing into white.

Chapter 10

For Kelly it was an act of survival.

When the single flame licked up against the sauna's fireplace glass, and the wood crackled and popped as a blaze consumed it — hope reignited, and with it a strong determination to escape. Heating the rocks was every bit a means of staying alive as it was staying in control when she felt so far from it.

Right now it was all she had to work with.

A warm glow spread throughout the small space. She was aware of how hot it would get over the next forty minutes, maybe too hot to remain inside, but there was a point to the madness.

"You can't stay in there," he'd said.

Of course not. He knew that, she knew that. The clock was ticking. Eventually, she'd have to emerge and run but that relied upon more than just aimlessly wading into the woods. Panic had killed many a hiker in the wild and

Kelly had no intention of becoming a statistic.

No, she needed time.

Time to plan.

Time to outsmart him.

She stoked the fire and threw in another log, all the while wondering if he'd burst through the door. Kelly removed her winter jacket and placed it on the cedar bench beside her and stared at the single exit.

Where was he?

What was he doing?

Was he out there, watching, waiting for her?

I don't want to hurt you. His words echoed in her mind.

Words that sickened her. She didn't believe him for a second. He'd already lied more than once, already shoved her into a counter. If he didn't want to harm her, what was his end game? Why was he here? Was this all part of toying with her? Most importantly — who was he? Did Cole know him? Was this some kind of twisted form of retribution? No. Cole liked to be at the helm of abuse. It was about power, control. It had been one of the main reasons why he became a police officer. Of course not all cops were like that but it was clear that some enjoyed it, and pushed the envelope of what was allowed.

Kelly inched toward the door and peered through the frosted pane of glass. Snow fell heavy and thick, blurring the trees and lookout. The wind howled loudly making it hard to hear anything except the blood in her ears. A light from inside the lookout glowed a dull yellow. She squinted. Was he in there? Her vision was limited. The small window was only meant to let in a few rays of daylight. If it was too large, a lot of the heat would have escaped. Her eyes drifted to piles of wood up against the outhouse.

The axe. She'd left it beside the sauna. If she could just get out and grab it, then… She sighed. No, that's what he wanted. As soon as she opened that door he would pounce. He was out there, waiting.

* * *

Erin rubbed her hands together to stay warm. The

heater in the Snowcat wasn't strong. It was a makeshift unit that Hank installed below the front seats, mostly to keep the feet of guests warm in the back. Bundled up in a dark black winter coat with thick boots, gloves and snowshoes at the ready, she tried to get her bearings. Every tree looked the same, coated in white. "Hank, I really appreciate this. I think my 4WD would have made it but Bryce was worried I'd get lost or stuck, and with the spotty cellular activity, well, thanks for the ride."

Hank gripped the steering wheel tight. The windshield wipers pumped back and forth, a steady rhythm that was hypnotic. Two bright headlights cut into the darkness revealing the wintry deluge. Hank waved her off. "Oh don't mention it. I told Kelly I would bring up some more logs. I was going to do it tomorrow because of the weather but then you called… and, well I can kill two birds with one stone. Besides, it gives me a reason to get out of the house. Mrs. Walton is on the warpath at the moment."

Erin laughed. "Marriage that good?"

"Yep, thirty-two years. You have a lot to look forward to."

The Snowcat rumbled over compacted snow, its tracks making easy work of the storm as it came up on the final stretch.

"So what trouble have you ladies got planned?"

"C'mon now, Hank, you know we can't tell you," she said with a smile before reaching into her bag and pulling out a bottle of Chardonnay. "I figured she deserves a night off from it all."

He nodded. "Very nice. That's good of you." He was quiet for a second or two, before he glanced over. "This isn't because of guilt, is it?"

Erin looked at her. "That obvious? Did Kelly say anything?"

"No but you know how people talk. And well…"

She groaned. "Yeah, they can't stop flapping their gums in this town." She squinted. "Look, I would be lying to say I don't feel somewhat responsible."

"Don't be so hard on yourself. You didn't know how

he would turn out nor did Kelly. I'm pretty sure most folks don't know where it will end up when they enter a relationship."

Erin shrugged; her coat rustled. "I know but… I just wish I had a way to turn back time."

"You were trying to do the right thing, be a good a friend and whatnot."

Hank narrowed his eyes and looked as if he was having a hard time seeing but he'd driven this trail so many times, Erin was sure he could have done it with his eyes closed.

"Lining her up with an abuser. Yeah, that's a good friend."

Hank snorted. "Well she's out of it now."

"She's not out of the woods yet. Let's hope that asshole gets what he deserves."

The Snowcat's tracks bit into the snow and came to a halt at the bottom of the driveway which cut up into the forest. They leaned back in their seats as it began the climb. It couldn't go all the way, the last 10 percent had to be on foot but it managed to get up around the 90 degree bend before he parked it. "You need a hand with the logs?" she asked, climbing out as he cut the engine.

"No, go on up and get warm. I'll have this done in a New York minute."

Erin slipped into snowshoes and trudged up toward the lookout. In between the trees she could see its dull glow, like a beacon, a lighthouse shining its beam out, 360 degrees. Another gust of wind blew ice crystals into her face, making her gasp. The fur around her hood whipped into her eyes as she squinted. She cast a glance back to Hank but could only make out the dark form of the Snowcat.

Bryce thought she was crazy for going up there again, especially so soon after they'd spent the week there. He was a big-city boy and wasn't used to the wildness of northern Idaho, whereas she'd grown up in these parts, the woods were her playground. Maybe, that's why she'd encouraged Kelly to pursue the purchase of the lookout.

Ahead, all she could see was snow, blowing and

swirling as she made her way to the foot of the lookout. She looked down at her snowshoes pressing into the deep snow that had compacted since yesterday. She plodded on, removed them and grabbed the railing that led up to the hatch.

"This is going to be ice wine by the time we drink it, Kelly," she said under her breath. As she climbed the final steps, she was just about to knock when the hatch opened and a good-looking stranger loomed over her.

"You must be Erin. I'm Adam, Kelly's brother."

Her mouth widened and she remembered Kelly saying he would be coming up. "Oh, wonderful. She said you'd be visiting." He extended a hand and helped her in. He was a strapping fellow, chiseled chin, broad shoulders and wearing one of the jackets that had been hanging up on the door, one belonging to Cole. "Wow, it's blustery out there. I told Kelly I would be coming tonight. I'm meant to stay and have a few drinks," she said looking around hoping to see Kelly.

* * *

Kelly had been sitting on the bench contemplating what to do. The sauna was close to reaching full temperature except she hadn't splashed any water on the hot stones and she didn't intend to — that would have only suffocated her in a plume of steam and she had already stripped down to her pants and shirt. Even her boots were off.

Sitting there wasn't going to get her anywhere. She sidled up to the window and carefully peered into the frozen world of Mother Nature. Kelly feared that he would eventually attempt to smash the glass and try to unlock the door, but even if he did, unless he had arms like an orangutan, he wouldn't be able to reach the lock. The door rattled again, and for a second she thought he was there but it was just the wind beating against it, lifting snow and creating a tornado of white. It howled furiously, making it that much harder to hear if Travis was nearby.

Kelly touched the cut on her head, blood had caked her cheek.

Her skull was throbbing and every few seconds she would feel a jolt of pain course through her, the beginning of a headache, or perhaps worse — swelling of the brain. Her head had struck that headboard pretty hard.

The axe was around the side of the sauna, stuck into a log. All she needed to do was slip out and grab it. She could be back within less than a minute if she moved fast. Donning her coat and boots, Kelly carefully pulled the latch, making sure to not make a sound. Her stomach dropped, an ominous feeling of doom washed over her as she pushed open the door, ever so slowly.

* * *

Kelly's brother took the wine from her hand and placed it on the counter while looking for a corkscrew. Erin scanned the room. Everything looked in place. Nothing unusual.

"So where's Kelly?" Erin asked still standing, unsure if she should stay now.

"Oh she didn't say?" he asked over his shoulder as he

fished into the cutlery drawer.

"Say what?"

He turned with a corkscrew in hand. "She went into town with our mother earlier today. Yeah, said she might end up staying because of the weather."

He walked over to the window and looked out, and shook his head.

"You're joking, right? I told her that I was coming tonight."

He laughed then it faded. "I'm gathering you haven't met our mother then?" He bit down on his lower lip, his eyes darting to the window. "She can be pretty insistent when she wants to. I think that's where Kelly gets her stubbornness."

"Strength you mean," Erin said, quick to correct him. She didn't like the idea that anyone could make Kelly feel any worse than she did, even if he was her brother.

"Right," he nodded, holding the corkscrew in hand.

"She's been through a lot over this past year and the last thing she needs is anyone making her feel less than."

His lip curled. "Oh I hear you. No, I think her future is bright."

Erin looked around the room then at him. "I couldn't help but notice…" She pointed at his face and he let out a chuckle.

"Oh this." He sighed. "Yeah, Kelly warned me not to spend too long inside the sauna or get too close to those rocks. That steam is crazy. Really hot."

"Yeah, I was saying the very same thing to my guy."

"Is he here… with you? I noticed someone outside."

"Oh, no that's Hank. The caretaker of the lookout. He gave me a ride because of the weather. He's just bringing up wood now."

He rocked his head back and nodded. "Ah, right."

Erin blew out her cheeks. "Well this is inconvenient. I'm not sure if I should wait, or…"

"No. I'm pretty sure they said they were going to stay the night at the motel."

Erin took out her phone and looked at it. "And of course when you need reception you can't get it." She placed it back into her pocket, looked at him and smiled. "I wouldn't even know if she sent me a text."

"Yeah, pretty shabby reception up here." He shrugged. "What can you do. Look, I'll tell Kelly you swung by or maybe you can check the motel — that is if you catch her in time."

"What do you mean?"

"Well, she was thinking of heading back to Boise with our mother. I offered to wrap up things here. You know, winterize, close it down and so forth." He sucked in a lungful of air. "She's really going to miss this old place."

Erin's brow knit together in confusion. "Miss?"

"Oh she didn't tell you?"

Erin was even more perplexed.

"She's thinking of selling. Yeah, it's just a lot of work and a distraction from her writing." He leaned against the counter and took a deep breath, casting another glance outside as if he was concerned about the weather or something else.

"Huh? I always thought she loved this place."

"I know. Disappointing. I tried to talk her out of it but she seemed pretty convinced that's what she wants to do. Anyway, if I speak to her before you, I will let her know you dropped by. You do have a ride back, I gather?"

Still perplexed she only caught the end of what he said. "Ride. Yes. Hank. Well. It's nice to finally meet you. She spoke a lot about you."

"Good things, I hope?"

"Always."

She smiled as she turned and lifted the hatch and began to exit. As Erin dropped down to eye level with the floor, she noticed something unusual, a pot tucked under the bed, there was a puddle of liquid nearby, brown in color.

"You uh, drop a pan?" she asked.

"Oh, that. Yeah. My bad. Please, don't tell Kelly. I'm such a butterfingers. She'll ride me over it for weeks. I was cleaning up when you knocked. I just kicked it under the bed — you know, didn't want the place looking a mess."

She nodded. "I know the feeling. I'm usually flying

around our house picking up Bryce's socks and dishes when uninvited guests show up."

They both laughed and he followed her out.

Chapter 11

Was her mind playing tricks? Kelly could have sworn she heard voices, low, undistinguishable. Kelly tilted her head and closed her eyes in a concerted effort to focus. It was only a few seconds, but it felt like longer. Eyelids sealed shut, she heard nothing — no conversation — except the wind howling. Her eyes blinked open to the darkness of night and snow spinning up, wrapping her in a blanket of white. She was on the far side of the sauna, out of view of the lookout, and unable to see if he was coming. Latching on to the axe's handle, she tried to free it. It was harder than before. The cold had all but frozen it inside the huge log. All around her stacks of wood were wet and covered in snow. She pressed her boot against the edge of the log to gain some leverage, then cast a nervous glance over her shoulder before forcing her weight down. *C'mon!* It should have shifted but instead the log just rocked.

Damn it!

The wind nipped harder; her body was quickly losing heat.

A sudden barrage of ice needles stabbed her face as a monster gust of wind shook her violently. Kelly gasped as she lowered her head, trying unsuccessfully to free the axe. "C'mon. C'mon, you bastard!"

* * *

Erin turned and hollered into the wind as Kelly's brother remained on the lower step. "Well, hey, nice to meet you."

He smiled and nodded but seemed distracted by Hank who was hauling up an armful of logs and heading toward the sauna. "Oh, uh Hank, you can just leave those there. I will..." he called out but Hank didn't hear him. The noise of the 90 mile an hour wind, the rustle of the trees was too loud. Hank just thought he was waving and waved back, continuing to tramp toward the sauna where gray smoke billowed out the chimney. Why was it on?

"He's fine. He's just dropping off wood," Erin said,

distracted by the smoke.

Kelly's brother looked concerned; his expression seemed out of place. He bounced off the lower step into the snow and tried to catch up with Hank but because he wasn't wearing any snowshoes his legs sank. Perplexed as to why he was so bothered, she placed a hand on Adam's shoulder. "Everything okay?" she asked.

* * *

Using every ounce of strength to dislodge the axe, Kelly gripped the axe further down the handle and lifted the entire log in an attempt to smash it against the rest of the stack. No good. It was too heavy. She tried again, placing one foot on the log and the other behind her, and forced the handle down to pry the axe loose.

Finally!

In one sudden, jerking motion, the blade broke away and she turned to head back into the sauna.

Too late.

Kelly heard the slosh of boots in snow before she saw the figure, hood up, coated in white, coming around the corner with a handful of... Before she even registered what it was, she raised the axe and slammed it into the crook of his neck.

Logs tumbled.

One after the other they dropped into the snow as the hooded figure looked up, his face an expression of horror, caught in the grip of certain death.

"No. No! No. Hank!"

He looked at her with desperate eyes, unable to speak before stumbling back and dropping, blood gushing out of his neck turning the snow instantly red.

Frantically, Kelly dropped to his side and placed a hand into the bloody crook of his neck. The axe was stuck deep in the bone, instantly her hands were gloved in red as she struggled to find words. Tears erupted from the corners of her eyes.

"I didn't know... I..."

His eyes glazed over, dull and expressionless as his spirit departed.

Falling on top of him, her tears got the better of her as

she wailed.

Then she realized. Where was he? If Hank had made it here in one piece, had Travis left, escaped while he could? It was possible. Fishing into Hank's pockets, her eyesight blurred by tears, and coughing because she was hyperventilating, Kelly searched for his cell phone.

Gripping it tightly she looked up at the sight of movement off to the left. A blur of darkness. Hurrying through a curtain of snow, Erin came into view, rounding a cluster of trees, her eyes widening in shock at the grim sight. "Erin!" She looked back at Hank. "I… I…" Words failed her as she tried to get a grip on the situation. Shock was taking over, adrenaline pumping through her body, making it hard to think.

Erin stood there speechless, her eyes bouncing between Kelly and Hank.

That's when a dark figure emerged from behind her.

Kelly cried out, "Erin. NO!"

Too late.

Travis punched the corkscrew into Erin's neck,

twisting it and staring at Kelly. Erin's jaw widened, no words escaping her lips. Her knees buckled even as Travis continued to screw the metal into her neck while his other hand held her head.

Though she was having difficulty breathing and controlling a runaway heart, Kelly's survival instincts kicked in. She saw the sauna door, still a few feet away. Her only place of protection — from the elements, from him.

Travis yanked free the barbaric tool of death as if extracting a cork from a bottle; blood gushed down Erin's neck as his eyes darted to the door.

As if knowing what she was about to do, he burst forward at the same time she did. Everything in that moment slowed, like having tunnel vision she saw nothing but that door.

Kelly raced forward only see him at the last second.

She slipped in as he shot out a hand and grasped her long hair, jerking her head back. Kelly cried out as a frantic struggle ensued. She had one hand on the door handle, which she slammed closed on his arm, and the other trying to free her hair.

Wedged between the sauna rocks were long tongs used for picking them up. One end glowed a deep orange. Using every bit of strength she could summon, Kelly drove her feet against the ground and held the door against his arm while reaching out for the tongs. Screaming in agony, she extended her free arm. Her fingers raked the air, inches away from the handle. "C'mon!"

She slammed the door even harder causing him to release his grip just briefly. It gave her just enough space to latch on to the wooden handle. Snatching the tongs she brought the hot end down on his hand, searing his skin. It sizzled as Travis let out a gut-wrenching scream and yanked free his hand, allowing her to force the door shut and drive the lock home.

As she looked at him through the tiny window, Travis drove his hand into the cold snow for relief. His head tilted back, his mouth widened as he writhed, his expression a mixture of pain and anger. He locked his eyes on her and rose to his feet, jaw clenched. Travis scanned behind him and tramped over to where Erin was. He picked up the corkscrew and waded over to the door. Holding the bloody steel between his fingers he pounded the window causing it to shatter, sending shards of glass all over her.

"It didn't have to be this way, Kelly," he said leering through the window. She could tell he was contemplating putting his hand through and seeing if he could reach the lock but she was still holding the scorching hot tongs in a threatening manner. He gritted his teeth and disappeared out of view.

A cloud of white whooshed through the opening, filling the inside with large snowflakes. Panting hard, trying to regain a breath, Kelly listened intently.

There was noise outside but she couldn't make out what it was.

Inching forward, careful not to get too close to the small opening, she peered out. *Where are you?*

Then without warning, he shot into view, wielding the axe that had been embedded in Hank's neck. *Crack. Crack. Crack.* Multiple times he struck the door. "One way or another you're coming out of there," he said between booming strikes.

The door was thick, really thick as she didn't want the sauna losing heat so she only used the best, but it wasn't axe proof. Even the thickest trees fell.

Think. Think. Think fast!

Her gaze darted to the hot rocks. Doing the only thing she could while trapped inside, Kelly latched on to a hot rock with the tongs and tossed it out the open window at him. Several missed but soon she hit the mark making him even more angry. One after the other she tossed the scorching rocks, forcing him back. He stood at a distance, waiting, axe at his side, blood dripping from its head, staining the snow.

"Why are you doing this?" he asked as if he was the victim. He genuinely seemed confused. She shook her head. He was mentally sick. He had to be.

"You killed her."

"She would have told."

"You killed her!" Kelly cried out with burning hatred. Tears flooded down her cheeks as she begged him to leave. "Just go. Go! Please!"

"I can't. You know I can't. Not after all we've been through?"

"What are you talking about? You're out of your mind," she croaked, her voice now even worse. Losing her temper she reached for more rocks and lobbed them out, each one glowing red. They sank into snow, hissing and releasing steam.

"Eventually you'll have to come out of there. You'll run out of rocks, you'll get hungry and..." He looked off to where Erin would have been. "And no one else is coming."

She couldn't believe how stupid he was. Did he really think that Hank's wife, or Bryce wouldn't worry? That they wouldn't come out themselves or call the cops? Her eyes darted back and forth, her mind making connections.

No, that's not what he was saying. He wanted them to come, he'd kill them just like he did Erin. Travis shook his head at her and walked out of sight. Kelly cautiously moved to the opening.

She heard him curse, losing his mind, crashing the axe into the logs before attempting to hack his way into the sauna through the far side wall. The sauna shook with every strike.

Not wasting time, Kelly pulled Hank's phone from her pocket and powered it on, hoping to God that it wasn't password protected. It took a few seconds before she was staring at the main screen. It wasn't locked. She breathed a sigh of relief and thanked God until she saw there was no signal. "No. No. No! Shit!"

Outside Travis continued his outburst of violence.

The wall echoed, the outside split and she knew it would only be a matter of time before he hacked through the first layer of paneled wood, the insulation and then the second layer.

She considered slipping out while he was going nuts but the chances of escape were low. Instead, she held up the cell phone and walked around trying to get a signal. "Give me one bar. One bar. Please, God. Please," she pleaded. She wasn't religious, a woman given to going to church or reading religious texts, but neither was she an atheist. Could she even get a signal inside the sauna? She'd never used a phone in there. With all the insulation, would it even work? She just needed one bar. To make a connection. To call the cops.

Kelly stared at the window and knew what she had to do.

She raced over and stuck it out, risking her own hand. If she hadn't heard him cracking the axe into the wall, she wouldn't have done it but Kelly figured he wouldn't see her on the other side.

Still, nothing.

"Please God."

More seconds passed.

Then as if by some miracle, one bar appeared.

Hope filled her chest, as she punched in the number for emergency services. Keeping the volume down as Travis continued pounding, her mouth went dry. "C'mon. C'mon," she said.

"Benewah County emergency services, operator 28, what's the location of your emergency?"

"Hello. Hello. This is Kelly Danvers."

"Ma'am, you'll need to speak up."

Her damaged voice and the howling wind were making it virtually impossible for the operator to hear Kelly. And yet she couldn't speak loud or Travis would hear, and she couldn't pull the phone into the sauna out of fear of losing the connection.

"Kelly Danvers," she cried out as loud as she could while keeping the phone close to the window. Right at that moment two things happened: The call dropped as the signal was lost, and Travis heard her. He came into view, wielding the axe.

Her hand shot in just as the blade crashed against the door inches from her.

Chapter 12

Half an hour earlier, Lucas Hurst knew he shouldn't have had that third cup of coffee. His heart was racing even though he hadn't exerted himself beyond patrolling the streets of Emery.

Outside the snow created a swirling tunnel before him.

His SUV windshield wipers were slapping back and forth at full speed and hardly making any impact. While he wasn't reading anything into his run-in with Kelly Danvers, he would have been lying to say that he didn't think there was something amiss with Cole's statement. He'd read it several times, and although it was plausible, something didn't ring true. Call it a gut instinct, an inner bullshit meter if you will, but Lucas liked to think he could sense when someone wasn't being truthful.

Having been an officer for close to thirty years he'd seen it all — the good, the bad and the ugly. It was all there. Cocky officers were notorious, and those that abused power were in every department in the country, even if their ability to keep their negative behavior on the down-low had been made more difficult since the introduction of body cameras. The losers still found ways around it.

Small-town departments really couldn't afford the cost of equipment. Body cameras were a great way to win the trust of the public but also a surefire way to burn through a budget, with some departments paying upwards of fifteen grand a year for equipment and video storage.

Still, there was always a smidgen of truth to rumors.

Over the past year, word had spread of Cole's misconduct. Of course, none of it could be substantiated but there was enough murmuring to give him cause for concern. Some of it was run-of-the-mill stuff, internal workplace bullying, one accusation of unwanted sexual advances, but mostly it was being a little heavy-handed with locals.

Perhaps that's why Lucas decided to roll past his home later that evening.

For someone who was meant to be hunting, he sure left a lot of lights on at his home. He drove past a few times before pulling into the driveway. He figured if Cole asked, he'd say the visit was one of concern for his state of mind, and that he knew how separation could send people over the edge.

No sooner had he got out of his vehicle than a door opened. His familiar face, one slightly less clean cut than in weeks gone by, peered out.

"Lucas?" Cole asked, squinting into the whiteout conditions.

The weather was unforgiving, swirling up ice crystals into his face as he jogged over, tilting into the wind. "Cole."

"Come on in."

He widened the door and Lucas entered a dimly lit home.

"Sorry about the mess." Cole picked up handfuls of mail, some of which was open, and set it down on the counter. Lucas glanced at it; most were from Kelly's agent.

"That's a lot of mail."

"Oh yeah, fan mail. You should see her inbox. I was meant to forward all that to her new address once I get it from her lawyer." He turned on a few lights to brighten the interior. The home was modest for someone of Kelly's fame. The neighborhood, though, was on the higher end. Cole was wearing a thick white sweater, black jeans and boots. He'd grown a full beard and looked a little red in the eyes as if having cried or consumed weed. "Everything okay?"

"Yeah, yeah," Lucas replied looking around the house. "Just thought I would swing by and see how you're holding up."

"Ah, well… things could be better but that's separation for you."

"And a heavy internal investigation," Lucas added.

"Right." Cole cleared his throat and motioned with a wave to head into the kitchen.

"Not hunting?" Lucas asked.

Cole tossed some empty microwave dinner boxes into an overfilled trash can. He tied up the bag and headed for the side door. "Ah, decided to return early, you know with the weather and all getting bad," he replied. A gust of wind blew in, bringing with it a fine layer of snow that fell a few feet from the door. Cole slung the bag out into the night and pushed the door closed. "Coffee?"

"I'll pass. Had a few too many."

"Oh, I hear you. Well, I was going to make something hot anyway. You don't mind?"

"Go ahead."

Lucas took a seat at the breakfast counter. A single plate with a few crumbs was in the sink nearby, along with several cups. The blinds were closed and there was a musty smell to the home as if no one had cracked a window in weeks. Nearby was a dog-eared copy of Kelly's novel, *A Call to War*. Lucas scooped it up and thumbed through it while Cole fished out a bag from the cupboard. "She wrote one hell of a book, didn't she?"

Cole cast a glance his way and frowned as if he didn't

like him touching it. "I guess. You read it?"

"Nope."

"Well, you're not alone. Might have sold millions but it's not everyone's taste."

"You?"

"Have I read it?" Cole asked, as if it was a dumb question. He leaned back against the counter and chuckled. "When would I have the time?"

"You know they carry it in audio."

"Expect they do," he said in an unenthusiastic way. Lucas set the book aside and surveyed the kitchen. It was modern: tiled floors, tiled walls, glass and oak cabinets and granite counters. The appliances were all top of the line. "Certainly afforded you a comfortable life."

"As does my job," Cole said defensively.

Lucas got the impression he didn't like living in Kelly's shadow. Although it wasn't his business, he was curious to see what he made of her success. A person could tell a lot about another by the way they handled the success of others even if they didn't think it was warranted. "Must be hard," Lucas said looking over at him.

"With what?"

"Kelly getting all that fan mail, all that attention. I certainly could see how that could get under your skin. Anyone's skin for that matter," he added, not wanting to directly point at him. He shrugged, turning to pour boiling water into his mug.

"It's short-lived. It will eventually go away."

"Really? I got the impression her book was only gaining momentum."

"Nah, that's where you'd be wrong," Cole said reaching for a spoon and adding some sugar. "Every book has a shelf life. Sure, you'll get a resurgence in interest if it gets turned into a movie but I doubt that will ever happen."

"Why not?"

Cole stirred; the metal clanged against the mug.

"Read the book. You'll understand."

"So you have read it."

He snorted, caught in his own lie. "No. I got the Cliff

Notes. You know, to stop Kelly from nagging at me that I never read or appreciated any of her work."

"Did you?"

"Of course I appreciated it. Look around you, this house wasn't paid for with my wages. You should know that."

A cop's salary wasn't as dire as he made out but then again, in comparison to a bestseller that was being touted as the next Great American Novel, maybe it appeared that way.

"You sound jaded," Lucas said.

Cole laughed into his drink. "Me? Please. It's just words on paper — heck, words on screen nowadays." He sucked air between his teeth and nursed his drink with both hands. "There might be a few gullible folks sucking down her words like Kool-Aid but where's the real payoff? Huh? The satisfaction of coming home and feeling like the decisions you made really helped people. Can't get that writing a book."

Lucas found his reply odd. "I don't know, books,

music, films... they make us think. In turn that can lead to change."

"Yeah, whatever," Cole said dismissively, thumbing toward the fridge. "You sure I can't get you a drink?"

"I'm fine." Lucas breathed in deeply. "So... what have you been up to? I can't imagine having all this time on my hands."

Cole took a sip of his drink. "Yeah, it screws with your mind but I stay busy."

"Doing what?"

He shrugged. "To-dos around the house. Things I never got to before. Surprising what you can get done when you have a little time on your hands."

"Yeah. I bet." Lucas stared at him. "By the way, you wouldn't have seen Kelly's dog, would you?" Cole screwed up his face as if confused. "Well, it's just because we got a report that the dog is missing."

"Huh. Go figure. No. Why? Is she back?"

When he didn't reply, Cole smirked. "She's up at the lookout, isn't she?" He ran a hand over his jawline. "Let me guess, she's blaming me, am I getting warmer?"

"Look, you don't know anything, do you?"

"No but I'll be the first to let you know if I do. But here's the thing, I've been too busy *fighting* for my career," he said in a firm tone. "You know that thing she tried to destroy. And then of course there is my reputation." He laughed. "Well, that's shot. No chance of getting that back."

"I wouldn't exactly go that far, Cole."

"No? That's because you have an exemplary, untarnished track record. I did as well until she walked into the station and turned the table on me. Can you imagine that? After all these years. After what I've done for her."

Lucas could hear the disdain in his tone.

It was to be expected with anyone going through a separation but his seemed more than normal. Nowhere in his response could Lucas hear any empathy or understanding for what Kelly had gone through. It was as if all he cared about was how this would look — which, to be fair to Lucas, he understood that. The only thing cops really had was their reputation. Lose that and their credibility was gone.

Lucas drummed his fingers. "I know. I read your statement."

Cole shook his head, looking off toward the window, lost in thought. "You know, Lucas, things used to be good between Kelly and me. Hell, I worshipped the ground that woman walked on but it wasn't enough. I was never enough. She always wanted more. It's amazing how a little fame can change everything."

"I don't know, it looked as if she was sharing the perks."

Cole looked back at him and chuckled. "What, this house? It don't mean anything. It's just stuff." He ran a hand over his lips and shook his head. "It doesn't mean anything without her and well, that ship has now sailed." He sighed.

If Lucas wasn't mistaken he almost sensed that Cole regretted what had taken place, whether that was because it was now affecting his career and freedom or because in hindsight he could he see his own faults, that was questionable.

"If it's any consolation," Lucas said trying to lift his spirits, if only to prevent him from harming himself, a common occurrence among divorced men. "People do go on to lead fulfilling lives after divorce."

"Great. Good to know," he said shaking his head as he set his cup on the countertop and asked if Lucas wanted something to eat.

Lucas' radio crackled and he lowered the volume. "You know, Cole, you're not the first to have marriage issues. Cops have some of the highest divorce rates. Not all are domestic violence related but…"

"I didn't touch her," he spat.

"Right. You said." He didn't want to get into it with him as he'd already seen how hot-headed he'd become down at the station the night they arrested him, before he was released on his own recognizance.

Again, his radio crackled, and this time Lucas needed

to answer it. He lifted a finger and got up and headed over to the doorway to be out of earshot. "Go ahead."

"We got an emergency call from Kelly Danvers. You'd asked to be notified."

"When?"

The dispatcher reeled off the time. It had occurred only moments ago.

He asked for specifics but was told that the call had dropped and she hadn't called back. Dispatch was unable to reach her. There was no mention of guns, or even danger, just that she'd called. Was it a real cry for help or just blowing off more smoke?

"All right," he said glancing at Cole in the other room. Was it possible that Kelly was losing her mind, jumping the gun, nervous that Cole was lurking around every corner when in reality he was doing the one thing he should and staying clear of her? "I'm on my way." After getting off he smiled at Cole and motioned toward the door. "Duty calls. Just wanted to make sure you were okay."

"Did dispatch say Kelly?"

"No."

"Lucas."

"Right now, Cole, doing what you are doing is best for you and her. I've got to go. I'll catch up with you later." As he headed out to the four-wheel drive SUV, he picked up the pace. As soon as he fired up the engine he looked back at the house and saw Cole standing in the doorway watching him. The vehicle let out a high-pitched whine as he jammed it into reverse and backed out. He didn't turn on the emergency lights until he was a good distance from Cole's neighborhood.

After his conversation with Cole, Lucas couldn't help but wonder if there was truth to what he'd told him. Had this whole event been nothing more than some meltdown by a woman overwhelmed by the fame that came with the release of her book? It occurred with celebrities all the time. It also wouldn't have been a first to have someone come into the department accusing a partner of abuse only to find out that the accusation was being done out of spite and they were suffering from mental issues. The lengths people went to when they were unhappy were unreal.

Still, Kelly didn't strike him as the kind of woman to do such a vindictive thing. He knew her long before she met Cole, and before she found success with her writing. She'd always come across as the same person — happy-go-lucky, generous with her time and money and more than willing to go to bat for a friend. That's why he gave her statement weight.

Whether Cole was behind it or someone else, that was to be determined.

Why lie? Well... that was that part he was having difficulty with.

The rest was to be decided by the court in due process.

Lucas glanced at the clock. On a good day it took a good twenty-five minutes to drive out to the lookout but in this... he looked out at the deluge of snow... it could take upwards of fifty minutes.

He switched on his high beams, lit up the snow-covered forest around him and roared into the distance. The roads were still unplowed, forcing him to go slower than usual. He cranked the heat and settled back for the dangerous drive up to the peak.

Chapter 13

It wasn't a lie. Adam Danvers had been called into work at the base in San Diego, but it was only to sign off on some paperwork. After, he caught a flight to Spokane International Airport, and then began the short drive down to Emery.

His arrival was meant to be a surprise. By now he figured Kelly was probably a little annoyed, expecting him to not show. He couldn't wait to see the look on her face.

Adam hadn't seen Kelly in over two years. Hell, he hadn't had a real vacation in that time. His work with the U.S. Navy was rewarding but time consuming. He often found himself away at sea for long periods. Being stuck on an aircraft carrier drifting somewhere in the Pacific Ocean had its moments. While it offered an experience that few could ever get, it did have some downsides. He'd nearly lost his mind the day he got the message from his mother to say that Kelly was in hospital because of Cole.

All he wanted to do was travel back and get his hands on him. It was probably for the best that he was on deployment as he would have likely wound up in jail for aggravated assault. As the older brother, and only sibling, he'd always been protective of her.

With only one year difference in age, he'd been there through her high school years, experienced all the ups and downs of teenage life, boyfriends and heartbreak. And while they'd bumped heads growing up, his relationship with her had only improved as they got older.

Hearing that she'd been nominated for a Pulitzer Prize was astonishing, but when he learned she'd won it, he couldn't have been more overjoyed. His little sister. Who would have thought she'd become a writer, and a bestseller at that?

Anyway, when he eventually got to speak with her on the phone after the incident, he'd encouraged her to head out to San Diego, stay with him and his girlfriend, Megan. They had a baby on the way and it would have been nice to have her there for the birth. With her line of work, Kelly could go anywhere and wasn't tied down to Idaho, except for the lookout, and well, Hank had pretty much proven he could run the place like clockwork. That's why he tried to convince her to sell it to him for a crazy low amount of money.

If anyone would have jumped at the chance, Hank would have.

As Adam drove the last leg of the journey he thought back to that conversation.

"Just let it go. You don't need the money," he said.

"I don't want to. At least not yet."

"Because you're afraid you won't write a second book?"

"I caught lightning in a bottle, Adam. It rarely happens. I need to be mindful of that and…"

"Not take any risks. But you know staying there is taking a huge risk. Being anywhere near him is a risk."

"So what… women everywhere who have been abused are supposed to just get up and run away, leave behind all they've known, just because that's the smart thing to do — the safe thing to do?"

"At least while he's still out."

She sighed.

It had always been hard convincing her of anything, and yet her refusal to back down was probably her greatest strength. She did things her way, she made shit happen… as Kelly so eloquently put it. *"You don't know him like I do. He has too much to lose, Adam, to try anything. I have a court order against him. The department has him under a microscope. If he even breathes in my direction they'll know. He'll be dragged in and won't get another shot. Besides, I'll soon know what's happening with the case."*

"And mom?"

"Mom wants me in Boise. You know her. If she had her way I would have never left home. No, I can't stay down there. It's just not right. I'm a grown woman… a Pulitzer Prize winner," she said poking fun at herself. She never took it seriously. Others might have been inclined to announce it any time they could, but not her. She took the whole writing career in stride. That's what he loved about her.

"Well think it over."

"You sound like mom."

He laughed.

"You know when I'm back on land, I was thinking it would be good if I came up there, spent some time with you."

"Adam. Really. You don't have to. I'll be good."

He chuckled. "I know you will but I want to. It will be like old times. You know, when dad built that treehouse."

She snorted. "Oh that thing." She paused. "That was something else."

"Yeah it was. Makes me wonder if that's why you want to cling to it. Because of him."

Silence followed.

"Perhaps."

"You miss him?" Adam asked.

"Every day. I still have his last voice message on my phone."

Their father, Bo Danvers, had passed away from prostate cancer four years ago. Both of them had been close to him. He was the kind of man that went to great lengths to let his kids know that he loved them. When Kelly had the idea to purchase a lookout, their father had been there to help. He spent the first month working with Hank and getting the place ready for guests.

"Anyway," Adam continued, "with the baby on the way, I kind of get the feeling that I won't have as much freedom as I do now."

"Please. Megan is the one who'll be up at night. You'll be out on the ocean, swigging whiskey with your guy friends."

"Oh yeah, because that's all sailors do."

They both burst out laughing and like that he was back in the present, squinting through a windshield of snow. Vast swaths of land to his right and left were empty of trees where loggers had eaten away the landscape. In the distance, snowcapped mountains loomed over numerous evergreens. He tried to make out the four-mile marker that indicated how close he was to the steep driveway that led up to the lookout. It was hard to see anything. He swallowed hard, gripping the wheel until his knuckles went white.

Adam had rented a Ford Bronco with 4WD, something he knew wouldn't have any problems tearing through snow and climbing the precarious terrain. Kelly had warned him about the steep driveway that really was only good for snowmobiles and ATVs in the winter. Another ten minutes and he spotted it. A small wooden sign at the base of the driveway which usually welcomed guests looked like a white match. He shifted into 4WD and began to climb. His body jostled in his seat as the tires bit into the snow and chewed its way up. The snow was so deep, the tires began to spin. Realizing he wasn't going to make it, he threw it in reverse and backed up, parking the Bronco at the foot of the driveway. Adam had seen the property in the summer, even then it held a challenge. Still, the rough road was actually one of the main reasons why Kelly had got the land so cheap.

He climbed out and donned a pair of snowshoes and reached in for his duffel bag which had a week's worth of clothes inside. He slung it over his shoulder and moved side to side to work out the tension from the long trip.

Oh, I'm gonna sleep well tonight, he told himself as he trudged over the snow toward the peak.

Adam pulled at his black North Face parka. He'd made sure to pack warm. It had been a long while since he'd needed this level of clothing. San Diego was beautiful and warm nearly all year, a far cry from the icy cold winters of Northern Idaho.

The only other person who knew he was coming besides his mother was Hank. Hank had told him that if he got stuck or needed anything, to give him a shout. He hadn't expected to see him at the lookout and yet that's where he found the orange Snowcat as he rounded a cluster of trees. It was almost hidden from view by the constant snow. It had streaked over rocks and trees, making them indistinguishable. Adam ran a glove over the powdery window and cupped a hand, his breath fogging up the glass.

There was no one there.

Adam gave the door handle a pull and it opened.

He shrugged, figuring Hank brought up wood and

Kelly was probably talking his ear off. He slammed the door shut and continued on up the slope as snow billowed around him, making it hard to see but a few feet ahead. His exposed cheeks stung. I hope to God you have that fireplace on, he muttered, keeping his head down and navigating through the dense forest.

* * *

Their bodies were now covered, out of sight, and would remain that way until spring or until wildlife uncovered them. Travis had just finished covering a thick trail of blood from where he'd dragged Erin's body into the forest when he spotted the figure wading through the storm. At first he thought it was an animal as it was hunched over, dark and quite large, but then he saw arms swinging. He blinked ice crystals out of his eyes and looked at the sauna. It had been a close call last time. He couldn't have a repeat of that.

As he took a few narrow logs that had yet to be chopped to size and jammed them up against the door to ensure she couldn't get out, Travis saw a lock to the side of the door. He recalled her saying that the structure had originally been a shed and like most sheds, there was always a lock on the outside, a way to keep the door from blowing open. It was perfect. He dropped the logs into the snow and pushed the lock across. He peered in and saw her at the rear staring back at him. "Seems we got company," he replied. "You call anyone on that?" he asked, noticing the phone in her hand. She clutched it tight, still fearful of him.

"Fuck you."

He smirked. "All in good time," he replied before taking another log and jamming it into the opening where the glass had been and shaking it a few times to check if it could be moved. He then took the two Adirondack chairs and piled them up in front of the door for good measure.

Next, Travis turned and looked toward the lookout. Through the trees he could make out the silhouette of the stranger inside. "Let's find out who you are."

* * *

After shaking off snow, and throwing back his hood, Adam stared around the empty abode. The light was on but where was Kelly? He glanced down and saw a pot and a large stain on the wood. Adam crouched and touched it. It was cold and wet.

"Kelly? Hank?"

Where could they be?

Then he remembered the sauna nestled in the woods down below. Would both of them have used it? He turned to head down when a face looked up at him.

"Howdy!"

"Hey," Adam said, a frown forming. "Kelly with you?"

"Gone into town with her mother."

He frowned. Only an hour ago he'd just got off the phone with her. She was in Boise. "I saw the Snowcat in the driveway. Is Hank around?"

The man emerged from the dark hole, he shook off snow and ran a hand over his frosted hair and wiped the icy buildup that had accumulated on his eyebrows. "No, he let me use it."

"Right. And you are?"

"Adam. Kelly's brother." The stranger extended a cold and meaty hand.

A shot of fear went through Adam as he shook the imposter's hand. It wasn't fear of him but of what had become of his sister, and Hank. "And you?" the stranger asked.

Adam reeled off the first name that came into his head, a friend back at the base — "Noah Griffin. I work with Kelly in the publishing industry. I'm one of her editors."

"Oh, really. That's cool. So what brings you up this way? Especially in this weather?"

"Well she mentioned she was working on a new book and she had written a few pages and wanted input."

"She couldn't email them to you?" the man asked.

"Out here? No Wi-Fi, right?"

"Right," the man said, narrowing his gaze and shifting his weight from one foot to the next. He looked uncomfortable, as if Adam was infringing upon his home.

"Besides, she has this weird superstition that if she

waits until the book is done before handing it over, that it won't do as well. She likes me to go through the first few chapters"

"Really?"

He rolled his eyes. "You know these creative types. Lucky socks, lucky pen... lucky editor."

"Lucky you," he said not taking his eyes off Adam for even a second. He leaned back against the counter.

Adam nodded. "Yeah, I guess so."

"So you from the area, Noah?"

He cleared his throat; his mind was already beginning to go through various scenarios of what he could do. He'd eyed the knife block on the counter, the short clothesline that hung down, and even considered throwing the guy back down through the hatch.

"Emery. I mostly work with other writers but I guess Kelly and I have this unique relationship. Yeah, there's not much I wouldn't do for her," he said.

"That makes two of us," he said back before smiling. "You are welcome to stay for a hot drink but I should let you know that she told me she wouldn't be back until the morning. Wants to spend some time with her mother before she heads back to Boise, actually."

"Which of course is where her mother is from," Adam added.

The stranger nodded. "Exactly."

"Huh. And there was I thinking that I was going to spend the next few hours poring over her latest novel. I was looking forward to it."

"Hot drink?"

"Sure." Adam concluded he could learn more about him and maybe where Kelly was if he just played along. The imposter closed the hatch and locked it and glanced at him with a thin smile before turning toward the stove. "Hot chocolate sound good?"

"Perfect."

"So, tell me, Noah. You just an editor?"

He swallowed hard. "A father, too, I have a young one on the way. In fact this works out good as I can get back to them tonight and follow up with Kelly on Monday."

"Yeah, you don't want to miss out on those precious moments. Life is so… fleeting," the man said, turning with a kitchen knife in one hand, and a photo of Adam on Kelly's phone in the other. "Don't you think, Adam?"

Chapter 14

Kelly stabbed the heavy-duty tongs against the end of the log in an attempt to pry it loose from the open window. She heaved, gritting her teeth. Pieces of bark crumbled, and slivers of wood split. As the log wedged into the opening wasn't an exact fit, and there were small uneven gaps surrounding the log, she tried to jam the steel tongs into the thin opening and pull down to widen it.

Who'd arrived? Was it the police?

She had screamed as loud as she could but no one came. Her voice was damaged seemingly beyond repair. She knew the only way to escape was to keep hammering away. That's when it dawned on her — Kelly dropped the tongs, and picked up a log similar in size. Gripping it with both hands, one on the end closest to her, the other on the side, she began to slam it against the log in the small square window. Pounding it relentlessly, she knew it was only a matter of time. More debris showered the floor. Her hands ached and burned from multiple splinters. "Damn it!" she said, dropping the heavy log. Kelly panted hard and picked it up again.

Another strike.

Two more, and then a shift.

That's it. It's working!

Just a few more inches and it would be out. Kelly took a step back and put her shoulder into it. The colliding noise was dull, like a mallet hitting the top of a flat object.

"I've. Had. Just. About. Enough!" she cried out between strikes. The final one did the trick. The log exploded outward, its landing soft and silent; a gust of freezing wind stole her breath.

It had been at least two minutes since Travis had disappeared. Kelly would have been overjoyed to have seen the log hit him square in the face as it shot out, but he was nowhere to be seen. Unsure if this was just a ploy, a means to get her to open the door, she cautiously inched forward and her head bobbed from side to side trying to get a bead on his whereabouts.

Between the trees, the tower loomed out of the white.

Had it not been for the glow of the lights she may not have seen him.

Kelly squinted. "Adam?"

Her eyes widened. He wasn't supposed to be here.

No, this wasn't real, her mind was playing tricks on her.

She blinked hard, hoping that when she opened her eyes it would just be a hallucination. It wasn't. Her stomach sank. At first Adam appeared to be alone, then Travis stepped into view passing by the window.

"No. No. NO!" Kelly cried out but he couldn't hear her. Even if the wind wasn't howling, her voice was a shell of its former self, nothing but a croaky, damaged box in a state of repair. "Adam!"

* * *

"Who are you? Where's Kelly?"

The stranger stared back, his head cocking to one side. No smile, barely a flicker of an expression. The man brought a finger up to the tip of the knife, twisting the handle ever so slightly, not taking his eyes off Adam for even a second. Already Adam was sizing him up, assessing options and the chances of survival.

"Answers. Everyone wants answers. It makes it easier, doesn't it? To sift the wheat from the chaff, the deserving from the undeserving, the righteous from the wicked. You don't want answers, you want to judge, to cast me aside so your life can continue without pain — but life is pain, Adam, without it we are nothing. It's a gift."

He was a lunatic; of that Adam was sure.

Adam shifted ever so slightly but the stranger registered it and mirrored him.

He lifted a hand and tried to reason with the stranger. "Look. We don't need to do this. Just tell me where she is."

The man wagged a finger at him then motioned to the bed. "Take a seat."

Adam frowned.

"Take a seat!" he said in a controlled but firm manner.

Adam took a few steps back, his legs bumping into the bed frame, but he was hesitant to follow orders. Sitting would place him at a disadvantage.

"SIT!" the man bellowed, losing his cool before taking a few deep breaths.

Reluctant, Adam sat. "What do you want?"

"Isn't that the question. What do I want? What does anyone want, Adam? Does it even matter?"

"Well maybe I can help you."

Communication had de-escalated numerous incidents in his career, and although the man before him looked unstable, it was worth a shot. The stranger snorted, shifting over to where the hatch was and standing on top, to make it clear he wasn't going anywhere. "Who else knows she's here?"

That's why he hadn't reacted, he wanted answers just as much as Adam did.

"So Kelly is here? Where is she? Is she alive?"

"Who else knows?"

"Just me."

"You're lying."

"I'm not."

The stranger replied, "I already know you weren't supposed to be coming. She told me."

"It was going to be a surprise."

He tutted and shook his head. "Lay face down."

Adam knew where this was going. "You don't need to do this."

"Face down."

He gritted his teeth, nodded slowly, then in an instant, exploded upward. The blade shot forward, slicing the air as he grasped the man's wrist. They collided and slammed backward then slid along the counter, toppling over the butane stove, the boiling kettle and two cups.

* * *

Kelly screamed as she helplessly watched the confrontation play out. In and out of view they went, crashing into the countertops and disappearing to the floor. She'd already unlocked the door from her side but it wouldn't budge. Using Hank's phone she turned on the camera, and set it face forward and angled it out the opening to see what Travis had done. There on the screen, the lock was in place, several logs wedged against the bottom of the door and Adirondack chairs after that.

Anger got the better of her and Kelly took a few steps back and smashed her foot against the door, hoping to dislodge and shake loose the wood. All the while she kept glimpsing the silhouette of the two struggling for control. Adam was putting up one hell of a fight. All she could do was hope he got the better of him.

Thud, thud, thud.

Kelly smashed her foot against the door.

Making no headway, she balanced on a bench with one foot, and set the other against the ridge of the stove, then she thrust an arm out the window and strained to reach the lock on the other side. "C'mon, c'mon! Damn it!"

It was too far down.

Refusing to give up, she took the forty-inch steel tongs and tried again. This time she was able to touch the lock.

A few unsuccessful tries later, stabbing, twisting and hammering at it, and eventually it caught and slid out. Pulling her arm back in, she dropped the tongs and went back to kicking the door.

The entire sauna shook. Every few seconds she would look out and see if the logs were free. One was out of the way, just two more to go. About to try again, she peered through the onslaught of snow up toward the lookout.

"Adam?"

There was no movement.

She couldn't see either of them.

Then, a figure rose up, appearing against the window, but it wasn't her brother. Travis smiled as he peered down and lifted a bloodied hand. Setting it against the pane, and letting it slide, smearing the glass.

"NO!"

Travis reached for the light toggle and turned it off, sending the lookout into complete darkness. Kelly fell back, tears welling up, her emotions getting the better of her. All the strength in her legs went out from beneath her and she buckled, hyperventilating. Why? Why was he doing this?

Her body heaved, unable to cope.

Seconds turned to minutes as she sobbed her heart out.

Torn and overwhelmed, she wanted to quit, but quitting wasn't in her vocabulary.

All the grief, sadness and excruciating pain wrapped together, quickly to be replaced by anger and a determination to survive. Rising to her feet, she calmed herself. *You can do this. You must do this.* Kelly returned to slamming her foot against the door.

As she was leaning out again, and taking another look with the phone — a hand grabbed her wrist.

Startled, she cried out, now engaged in a tug of war with Travis on the other side. He tried to pry loose the phone from her fingers by bending a finger back, causing her to cry out in pain. It didn't work. She managed to extract her hand and took several steps back just as he reappeared at the window, glaring. He threw the Adirondack chair out of the way, and kicked the logs free.

A cold chill washed over her.

Her eyes widened, seeing that the lock inside wasn't in place.

Kelly dove forward, slamming it to the right just as he pulled on the door.

It rattled. He tried again but it held strong.

They locked eyes, glaring at one another.

Words escaped her. She wanted to scream but her mind was so bombarded with stress it just went blank.

In a calm and collected manner he spoke, "It didn't need to be this way, Kelly. Just open the door and we can go back to normal." She couldn't believe he could be so cold.

"Why are you doing this?"

"I'm not doing anything, you are."

She shook her head in disbelief.

"Who are you?"

He closed his eyes and shook his head. "No. No. No. Don't go there. You know who I am. Don't play games."

For the life of her she couldn't remember. Either she

was suffering from some mental breakdown from her time with Cole or she'd met him at some point in her life when she was younger and forgotten. A boyfriend? She'd had several in college. Some of her relationships were short-lived, nothing more than a one-night stand. She usually was good with faces and names but with everything that had taken place, her ability to think straight had got progressively worse. The doctor had prescribed anxiety and sleeping meds — it was why she hadn't written a damn thing in two years.

"What do you want from me?"

"Open the door."

She shook her head.

"OPEN THE DOOR!" he bellowed louder, shedding his calm exterior and looking like a psychotic mental patient as he shook the handle. Seething, he took a breath, closed his eyes and then went back to acting calm as if nothing had happened. She'd never seen anything like it. It was like Jekyll and Hyde. Sure, Cole could be terrifying, but it still took him a few hours to calm down.

This guy could do it on a whim.

Travis replaced the logs and chairs in front of the door, and locked it again.

"Best I go clean up. We'll speak later."

She didn't even want to ask what happened to Adam; she already knew. The thought of it made her want to puke. Swallowed in grief, Kelly unleashed her anger.

"Is Travis even your name? Tell me!" she demanded to know.

He turned and walked away without responding.

Kelly charged at the door, shouting through the gap. "Who are you? WHO ARE YOU!?"

Travis vanished into the night, nothing but a dark blur.

* * *

The sight of the Bronco blanketed in snow didn't strike Lucas as odd or out of the ordinary. He figured it was Kelly's rental. The compacted snow crunched beneath his tires as he veered to the side of the narrow road and parked, letting his windshield wipers continue to clear snow as he stared up the driveway. With only four officers in the department, one sick, and the others busy with an upswing in accidents due to bad weather, pulling one away wasn't an option.

Beyond the odd domestic, Emery was fortunate to have a low crime rate.

The last murder had occurred over fourteen years ago, and that stemmed from an argument between two business owners.

His career in Emery had been a far cry from the busy shifts of city policing in Boise, back when he was a new recruit. Getting on in years, he kind of liked the slow pace. A few more and he would hang up the badge and retire to a life of fishing and people watching.

No, he figured he'd find Kelly safe and sound, with some excuse about having drunk one too many. She'd be apologetic, perhaps even slurring her words, or he'd find her passed out. While Cole wasn't a saint, Kelly also had a few skeletons in her closet. Lucas had pulled her over twice in the past three years after coming out of a bar and attempting to drive the short distance home. Initially she denied it but he could smell the alcohol on her breath, and if it wasn't for her husband, he would have arrested her. Instead, he used his discretion and opted to give her a lift home. It was around that time he learned from Cole that he was concerned about her drinking.

Lucas just thought it was a lie to cover up his own transgressions.

Of course it was a lot easier to believe a woman was lying if she had a drinking problem. Lucas pushed out, and turned on his flashlight. He collected his snowshoes from the back of the vehicle and slipped into them. He got on the radio and updated dispatch on his arrival before forging on through the snowstorm. He'd never been out to the lookout though he'd seen photos of the place on Cole's phone back when he and Kelly were on good terms. Cole loved to go on about his toys, his lifestyle and rubbing shoulders with the famous, as if he was somehow responsible when reality was he hadn't done a damn thing. He was living off the coattails of

Kelly's hard work.

Plodding up the driveway was a slog, deep snow, a steep incline — it was a reminder of how out of shape he'd become. In his early twenties, he'd been lean and had abundant energy. Where had it gone?

As he passed the Snowcat, Lucas frowned. What was Hank doing here? Maybe after hanging up on dispatch Kelly had contacted him for support. He trudged on; his mind lost in all the things he needed to get done that weekend. Policing Emery didn't require much thought. Unlike the city, not everything that looked out of the norm was cause for backup.

He hadn't made it halfway up to the lookout when he was approached by a hooded figure.

"That you, Hank?"

The stranger trudged toward him then shifted back his hood to reveal his face. "Nope, just me. I saw your lights and thought I would save you the trouble of the hike. One hell of a snowstorm, isn't it?" He extended a hand as he walked toward him. "I'm Adam Danvers by the way,

Kelly's brother."

Lucas shook it. He squinted into his frosted face. "Officer Hurst. We got an emergency call from Kelly."

"Yeah. I'm sorry about that." He lifted his hand as if indicating she'd been drinking then thumbed back to the lookout. "She's been under a lot of pressure recently. Thinks Cole killed her dog. Thinks he's out there watching her. I said I would keep her company."

Lucas looked around his shoulder and then directly at him, before nodding. "Yeah, I spoke to her yesterday. The dog not shown up?"

He breathed in deep and exhaled, shivering. "Unfortunately no. I went out looking today, found a little blood. I told her the dog probably was attacked by wolves."

Lucas cleared his throat. "You arrive today?"

"Yep, from Boise."

He nodded, giving him a skeptical glance. "Well, um, is Kelly around?"

"Actually no, she went into town with a friend of

hers." He stabbed a finger. "Erin?"

"Erin Miller?" Lucas asked.

The man clicked his fingers. "That's it. Yeah, for drinks."

Lucas glanced at his watch. "Didn't you think she's already had enough?"

"Of course, I tried to tell her but she wouldn't listen. Anyway, Erin said she would look after her. They've been out a while. Probably didn't even go to the bar. I imagine they've gone to Erin's place. Anyway, I said I would keep an eye on the lookout. You just never know who could show up, right?"

Lucas nodded, not taking his eyes off him. "Right. I saw Hank's Snowcat. He here?"

"Was here. Yeah. He caught a ride back to town in Erin's vehicle. Said I could keep the Snowcat tonight just in case the weather got worse."

Lucas jerked his head. "So the Bronco. That's your vehicle?"

He pursed his lips and nodded.

"Well, I'm out here now, I should probably take a look around," Lucas added.

"Not much to see," he said gesturing to the weather. "But by all means, come on up."

Lucas looked past him again. The light was on in the lookout and there didn't appear to be anyone inside. He also didn't seem very worried. The weather was bad, and not improving. "Well, just a quick look."

"Sure."

They ambled together up to the lookout, keeping their heads low from the howling wind. It was hard to see much of anything. "I don't know why she keeps this place open in the winter. I told her to sell it," he said, raising his voice. "Thankfully, she's agreed. She'll be heading out with me when I leave."

"Leaving Emery for good?" Lucas asked casting a glance around. A curtain of snow had made visibility low. The continued barrage of driving snow with high winds made it hard to breathe.

"Yep. Don't be surprised if she doesn't say goodbye."

Lucas pulled a face. "Well I hope you aren't afraid of heights," her brother said, patting him on the shoulder. "Mind your step, I had a bit of an accident the first time I came here in the winter," he said leading the way.

Lucas grimaced and second-guessed going up. "You know what," he said looking around again. "Tell Kelly I will speak to her later."

Her brother thumbed over his shoulder. "You don't want to come up?" he asked looking down from the steps.

Lucas waved him off. "Nah. It looks as if everything's fine," he said giving one more scan. Truth be told, hearing that she hit the bottle before making the call, and had now gone out with Erin to the bar, made sense. While he couldn't recall if she smelled of liquor yesterday, he had to wonder if she'd been drinking. The accusations toward Cole killing her dog seemed unfounded — maybe even a little neurotic. "Look, sorry to bother you. If you see Kelly before I do, let her know I dropped by."

"I will do, officer. Thank you. Safe journey back."

Lucas gave a small salute before retracing his steps.

When he'd made it back to the road, Lucas hopped in the SUV, and was about to fire it up when he glanced over at the Bronco. Call it a gut instinct or routine, but he decided to run the plates. They came back registered to a rental place out of Spokane International Airport. Boise to Emery was at least six hours' drive in good weather, it would have made sense to fly into Spokane which was only an hour and a half away.

He took out his cell phone and considered calling the bar but noticed no signal.

Lucas looked down at the radio.

Police radios worked even when cell towers didn't.

Priority, reliability, disasters, talk-around and ruggedness were just a few of the reasons they continued to use them. It was why cops carried radios that cost thousands of dollars vs. a cheap cell phone. Using a dedicated network, they wouldn't run into busy lines and in a disaster if a cell phone network collapsed, police and EMT would still have a reliable means of communication. Lucas sighed, and got in contact with dispatch. "Hey,

Debbie, do me a favor. Place a call to Logan's Bar, would you. Find out if Erin Miller or Kelly Danvers is there. If not, call Miller's home. Keep it casual. Nothing to worry about. Work your female magic."

It was things like this that they could get away with in a small town. There would be hell to pay if he did it in the big city. Something to do with tying up lines and whatnot.

"Will do," she replied.

He sat there catching up on paperwork, looking up occasionally.

A few minutes later, Debbie got back to him.

"Lucas, the bartender hasn't seen either one all night, and I phoned Miller's place and spoke to her partner, Bryce. Says Erin was supposed to be staying at the lookout with Kelly tonight. The last time he spoke to her was early this evening on her way out there with Hank."

"She left with Hank?"

"By the sounds of it, yeah. He gave her a ride."

He remembered what Kelly's brother had said when he

asked about Hank. *He caught a ride back to town in Erin's vehicle. Said I could keep the Snowcat tonight just in case the weather got worse.*

Why the discrepancy?

"All right, Debbie."

"You need anything else?"

"No, I'm good." He sat there for a moment pondering. He considered calling for backup but there was probably a good explanation. Kelly's brother had said Erin had left in her own vehicle, and yet Bryce said she went with Hank. If that was the case, how did they get back? He could have had Debbie call back but he didn't want to send Bryce into a panic. Also, Lucas wasn't one for jumping the gun, especially when it came to Kelly who already had come across as a little unhinged. He looked out at the dismal weather. With the way the snow was coming down, it would take another officer a good hour to reach him, and pulling them away if everything was okay would only place an unnecessary strain on their limited resources. Still, something didn't feel right. "Hey,

Debbie," he continued.

"Go ahead."

"Any of the officers tied up right now?"

"Not at the moment."

"Have a couple join me at the Danvers residence," he replied before reeling off the address. With that in place he got out of his vehicle with the intention of going up and having a few more words with the brother.

Chapter 15

The door exploded outward with one final kick.

Wielding the tongs like a baseball bat, Kelly exited ready for a fight, and with only one goal in mind — getting as far away from this place as possible. She expected him to pounce, to strike out of nowhere, as he must have seen or heard her repeating the same thing she'd done before — unlocking the door, using the tongs to push the Adirondack chair out of the way, then kicking until the stacks of wood dislodged.

But he wasn't there.

When she stepped out, the perfectly covered deck didn't even have prints.

Large snowflakes rushed down, heavy and thick, she breathed them in, each one melting on her tongue.

* * *

Beyond the trees, out of sight, Lucas knocked on the hatch door. "Mr. Danvers?" There was no answer. He pushed up the door expecting it to be locked but it flipped wide into darkness. "Mr. Danvers?" Where was he? With the floor at eye level he clicked on his flashlight before entering. The beam washed over the flooring and fell upon the bloody face of a stranger. His neck had multiple knife wounds. "What the hell…"

"You shouldn't have come back," a voice said off to his right.

Before he had a chance to shine the light on him, Lucas felt hot liquid hit his face. He screamed in agony, slipped and lost his grip on the ladder, falling to the second level of the lookout. He groaned in pain, writhing around as the heat from the liquid intensified, burning his skin. Lucas frantically slapped cold snow on his face but it did little to cool it.

Boots hit the floor nearby.

"Hot oil. Now that's got to be painful."

Lucas reached for his gun but before he could grasp it, his hand was smashed with something hard, shattering the bones instantly. He cried out as the man tutted.

"Now now, officer, let's not do that."

Though the pain was beyond anything he'd felt, Lucas' will to survive was far stronger. He twisted and kicked the man's legs out from beneath him before scrambling to attack. Blinded by the oil in his eyes, Lucas tripped and went over the unprotected edge straight into the snow far below. Swallowed by white, buried in three feet of snow, he struggled to get up.

Every breath felt like he was sucking in water. Scrambling, trying to right himself, he felt like a tortoise stranded on its shell.

Then, something solid struck him in the back.

He cried in pain, only to feel it again seconds later.

"This is gonna be a very bad night for you, officer."

* * *

It was a bloodcurdling cry cutting through the howling wind that made her turn back. Kelly squinted into the storm. She'd fled into the forest and maybe she would have got away if it wasn't for the repeated cries. Was it him? Had cops come to help? Or was he inflicting even more pain on someone else she loved? Perhaps it was Adam. Alive. Maybe he didn't die. Maybe he was fighting back. She glanced away, the thought of running was strong. But she couldn't. She had to know if it was her brother. Turning back, Kelly hurried through the wall of white to see.

As she emerged from swirling ice crystals, Kelly saw Travis looming over a figure, pounding them from behind with a mallet. Wielding the tongs she came up from behind him, her approach masked by the wind and snow. She lashed out, striking him as hard as she could around the top of the head.

Travis buckled, going down and no longer moving.

There before her was Officer Hurst, unconscious, his head and back covered in blood.

"Kelly," Travis groaned.

Her eyes bounced to him.

She hadn't hit him hard enough.

He lunged at her and struck her in the leg, just to the right of her knee. Kelly screamed and hobbled to the lookout. Scrambling as fast as she could, she ascended the steps, casting a glance over her shoulder and watching as Travis waded through the snow toward the staircase, mallet still in hand. Fear shot through her as she hurried up, slipping and smashing her knee into a step on the way. Tears streaked her cheeks, freezing as they fell, hope leaving her body as quickly as heat.

"This is your fault, Kelly."

His words could have been Cole's.

So many times she'd heard him say the same thing. Twisting around situations, justifying his reasons for hurting her. How often had she let him get away with it? It was a crushing blow to her self-esteem.

She was limping, struggling to climb, and Travis was gaining on her.

Thoughts of what he would do if he got his hands around her neck pushed her on.

Keep moving. Don't stop. Get up in that cabin.

She scrambled inside, her fingers clawing forward. She slipped on the oily floor as she tried to shut the hatch.

Travis was nearly up, almost upon her when she slammed the door down in his face and pushed home the lock.

Boom. Boom. Boom.

He struck the hatch underneath with the mallet over and over again,

Each time her body shifted as she sat on top, panting hard and trying to catch her breath. "Open up. Kelly. Open up!"

"Go away. Please!" she cried out, begging, pleading for him to leave her be.

"I can't. I won't."

As she sat there keeping her body weight flat, her eyes surveyed the room. *Adam?* Beneath the bed, on the opposite side, his eyes stared back, empty and without life. Tears overflowed as she scrambled toward him, throwing herself on top, checking his pulse with two fingers.

His body was cold.

He was gone.

She clutched his clothes and screamed into his neck.

"I'm sorry. I'm so sorry," she repeated over and over as if somehow she was to blame. Was she? Had she brought this upon herself? Travis seemed to think so. He knew her but she couldn't remember him. It was like she was trapped in a nightmare, reliving every emotion she'd gone through with Cole but now dialed up to eleven in intensity.

The drum of banging continued as Travis tried unsuccessfully to bust his way inside. Sitting there with her dead brother she went into shock, her eyes staring at the door, waiting, expecting Travis to burst in and end her life. A sense of hopelessness, the same overriding emotions of being victimized, tortured her mind and stripped her of what little courage remained. Kelly looked at Adam and remembered the conversation she'd had the night when she was still in the hospital.

For the first few minutes she did nothing but sob.

After she'd drained her well of tears, Kelly listened to Adam build her up just as he had always done before when she was a kid. "Don't you dare let him strip you of who you are. You are strong. You hear me? You are stronger than this. Stronger than anything he can do. You understand? It's okay to cry. But then get up. God damn it, get up!"

Like a light switching on, Kelly stopped crying.

Numbness kicked in, ridding her body of what tears were left.

Even as the booming of the mallet reverberated, she wiped her cheeks with her forearm and began to think. How could she get out of this? She wasn't dying here. She wasn't becoming a victim to another lunatic. Not here. Not now!

That's when the booming stopped.

She heard footsteps descending

Then it went eerily quiet.

She cocked her head.

Where have you gone?

Kelly looked up at the lightbulb. She crossed the room and smashed it above her, glass rained down. "You want to play games? Okay, you bastard. Let's play," she muttered.

Chapter 16

Cloaked in darkness, Kelly waited for her moment to strike.

It was no longer a matter of *if* he would kill her, only when and how. In the nervous silence, a cold chill overshadowed her. She couldn't hear him. No boots on the staircase. No voice. Just the sound of a howling wind. Where are you? Why me? Why now?

The questions bombarded, reminding her of every question she'd asked over the past three weeks. Lying in wait, ready to pounce, Kelly's mind drifted to the past, to better days with Cole. What had been the catalyst to set him off? He hadn't always been so possessive or violent. When she'd met him he was far from it. It wasn't like stress was a factor. He loved his job, and working as an officer in Emery was laid back. It was easy work, he'd say. He'd always told her how his shift was often spent cruising around, or parked behind the convenience store doing paperwork. Most of the conflict he'd encountered was internal, red tape, office politics — the usual crap.

Boredom. Initially that's what she notched it up to.

It wasn't like it happened overnight.

Things escalated, little by little.

Harsh words instead of kind ones.

Belittling instead of encouragement.

Outbursts instead of holding his tongue.

He was bored with the job, of that she was sure but he didn't want her to know that, he didn't want to feel less than he claimed to be. So… when her writing career took off, it pained him to see her living the high life, getting calls from media and jet setting around the country. *Attention.* That's what he'd craved. That was what he'd wanted. The acclaim. The praise. The thing that he thought police work would give him.

It hadn't.

Sure, he was loved by some in the community but like he said, people didn't see him, they saw the uniform, and what that represented.

That's when the drinking started.

That was the tipping point.

No longer did hurtful words suffice.

Of course he was always apologetic after. Pleading, crying, trying to get her to understand that it was the drink, not him. There was always a reason. A bad day at work, jealousy, insecurities, the list went on. And he always promised to never do it again.

Like many others, she believed her partner.

She wanted to see the best in him.

She wanted to think that things could get better, that they could be better people.

She didn't want to believe that her marriage would end in such a clichéd way.

Huddled in the corner, Kelly reflected on every chance she'd given him to turn things around but eventually she just stopped trying, stopped believing that he was capable of anything more.

She deserved better.

There was someone out there that would treat her with

kindness.

Lost in her thoughts she barely noticed the sound, it was just one of many around her, mixed in with the wind. Her body shivered; fear, stress, cold, grief, all of it was beginning to take its toll on her.

There, a shadow emerged over the edge of the railing, a few feet from her.

Instead of coming through the hatch, he'd opted to climb up and over.

Oh, you're determined.

Careful, ever so careful, his movement like a professional acrobat balancing on a beam, cautious that any sudden movement could topple him. Travis set himself down and peered through the frosted, fogged-up window. But it was too dark. There was no light inside. He had to enter.

The handle dropped so slow that not even metal could be heard sliding.

Then, Travis pulled the door hard. He opened it wide and burst in swinging the mallet, crashing it against anything that got in the way. "Kelly!"

Unseen, she moved, closing the gap between them.

She tightened her grip on the red fire extinguisher.

The pin had already been pulled.

"Kelly!"

He yelled again before turning her way.

As quick as a flash she exploded upward, squeezing the device that ejected a cloud of white powder in his face, caking his eyes, filling his mouth and causing him to gag and splutter. The entire enclosure filled with a plume of dry chemical.

Once it was emptied, Kelly wielded the metal tube like a bat, swinging it upward and connecting with his jaw. He exploded backward into the thick cloud, disappearing in a heap. She might have continued the assault if she could have seen where he landed.

Coughing hard, she dropped the extinguisher and dashed toward the hatch. As soon as it was unlocked, she climbed down, shutting it above her, locking it from underneath. If he wanted to get out now he would have to drop twenty-five feet into snow, or climb over the edge.

Frantically she hurried, her imagination and fear playing out the worst-case scenario. Her heart thumped in her chest and pulse raced as she dropped to the bottom and waded through thick snow to where Officer Hurst lay.

Rigor mortis had already begun to set in when she searched for a gun.

It was gone.

Shit.

Kelly rifled through his pockets and found a set of keys.

Yes. Yes!

A gun cracked above her; a bullet snapped past her cheek. She felt the wind inches from her skin. Not even looking up, she knew who it was.

The realization electrified her to the core.

Kelly rolled to her left, and scrambled up. Adrenaline kicked in, forcing her on, away from the bloody mess of

Hurst's pulverized remains. Several more bullets followed in rapid succession, one nicking her shoulder. Kelly cried out, feeling the unfamiliar but overwhelming sting of pain. She clung to her shoulder and pressed on, struggling to move from side to side to avoid another round but fortunately he didn't fire again. The tornado of wind and snow must have hidden her.

The last thing she heard was him crying out her name.

Her legs plunged into the icy snow, soaking her clothes and skin. Without snowshoes every step was harder than the last. *Run, run,* she told herself, but it was almost impossible. It felt like she was wading in knee deep quicksand, every step butting up against an unmovable force.

Sweat trickled down the small of her back, her breathing labored, just a series of desperate gasps, giving her the feeling that she was drowning in the thinnest of air. She lifted her feet, high, leaping steps across the deep snow trying to avoid sinking. She had no idea if Travis could see her. She wouldn't risk for even a second a look over her shoulder. Had he dropped, or found another way down? She wouldn't be able to tell if he was following as the noise of the wind and the muffling powder beneath her made every step silent.

Kelly harnessed her adrenaline, swallowed fear and picked up the pace to get down to Hurst's vehicle. It had to be there. She would call the department. Or had he already done that? The thought shot through her mind. *Please. Please have called for backup.*

Seeing the police SUV was so overwhelming, such a beautiful sight, that she almost cried in joy. Seconds from now, mere seconds and she would be inside, safe, away from him. Slipping and sliding on the compacted snow, she reached the door and pressed the key fob. It bleeped and she yanked it open. A thick layer of snow covered the windows making the inside even darker than the night. She got in, slammed the door and locked it. Her fingers were red and rigid from the cold. There wasn't just one key on the chain but several, probably one for his personal vehicle, a locker at work and a home key. It was so hard to see in the dark. She stabbed the ignition with one key only to realize it was the wrong one, two more attempts before she found it. It slid in and she turned over the ignition. It coughed to life the first time.

Hope erupted.

She grabbed the microphone for the radio and attempted to reach dispatch while at the same time engaging the windshield wipers. They burst into action, sliding a heavy load of snow to the left to reveal Travis, twenty feet away, coming down the slope as fast as his legs would carry him.

Panic speared her heart.

He raised the gun and fired two rounds through the windshield, sending shards of glass over her. She gasped in shock, her eyes widened as she jammed the gear stick in reverse and smashed the accelerator to the ground. The SUV shot backward, then spun out almost going into the tree line. She stabbed the brake and it slid out of control before stopping.

Travis managed to reach her before she could hit the

accelerator and tear out of there. He used the butt end of the gun to smash the window beside her. He lunged forward, grabbing her by the hair as she crushed the accelerator. The SUV lurched forward, the wheels biting snow and the engine roaring loudly as it peeled away.

He was holding on to her, and the vehicle. Kelly twisted the steering wheel trying to shake him loose. A clump of hair came out and he disappeared out of view.

Yes!

She glanced in the rearview mirror just as he fired three more rounds, shattering the windshield behind her and causing her to jerk the wheel erratically. A lack of traction and a sudden change in motion sent the SUV sliding off the road and crashing into the closest tree. Her head smacked against the side of the vehicle and she groaned in agony as the airbag exploded open, forcing her head back against the seat until it deflated.

Dust settled.

The horn rang out, one continual blare.

With blood running down the side of her face, Kelly

immediately opened the driver's door and slumped into the snow. The vehicle had come to an abrupt stop at an angle, with the passenger side facing Travis who was now slowly making his way over, slipping and sliding like someone trying to cross an ice rink.

She wanted to throw up, and lay there forever, but she couldn't.

Kelly thought she'd heard her brother's voice. *You're not dying here, get up!*

Groaning, lost in the dark, she scrambled away, limping now even more than before. "Kelly!" Another round erupted. Travis cried out but she didn't stop to look back. Keep moving. Keep moving, she told herself.

Move it! One foot in front of the other, Kelly ignored the pain in her thighs. Her lungs were burning as she fled through the forest, stumbling over hidden tree roots and boulders. Wheezing, she leaned against a tree, desperate to steal a breath. Her heart hammered in her chest as she heard him calling her name.

"Kelly, come back here. I don't want to hurt you."

Oh no, just firing the gun on a whim? She thought.

He wouldn't give up, and if he managed to capture her she was as good as dead. She pressed on, forging through snow; low-hanging branches raked her cold face, slicing her razor thin. A crack of a gun and tree bark exploded nearby.

She threaded around trees, stumbling and then scrambling to her feet. The pain in her shoulder was excruciating, and her knee felt like it was twice the size. It was hard to tell if she was heading further away from the lookout or circling around. Everything looked the same in those dismal woods. Her thighs screamed in protest — stop, rest, catch a breath, but she couldn't. She struggled to control the panic. Hunted. Was this what it was like to be hunted?

Another round tore up the nearest tree.

Her thoughts muddled, stress taking over.

For someone who didn't want to hurt her, he sure as hell was trying his best to stop her. She didn't want to die out in these dark and gloomy woods. She didn't want to join Erin, Hank, her brother and Hurst, just a victim of a maniac. She had so much to live for. It couldn't end here; she wouldn't let it.

So preoccupied with avoiding the barrage of gunfire, she didn't look at what was up ahead. Her foot hit a log covered by snow and she toppled over, landed hard, her knees driving into the earth, into rocks beneath before rolling down a steep slope.

With nothing to slow her, she went head over heels, twisting and turning, plowing through powdery snow and getting it stuck in every crevice of her body before slamming into a tree. She let out a groan and wiped the wet snow from her face.

Travis' voice echoed off the trees. "There's nowhere to go, Kelly. Come back here."

She grasped at the frozen underbrush sticking up through the snow like raised fingers and pulled herself upright. As she limped away, blood seeped into her eye from her forehead and droplets stained the snow behind her. She tried to cover her trail to prevent him from following but it was no use. Agonizing pain coursed through her, from head to toe. Now her ribs ached.

Overwhelmed and struggling for breath, she scanned the terrain. *I just need to find a place to hide... somewhere I can catch my breath... somewhere I can get my bearings.* Kelly pushed on, stumbling every few feet, her clothes torn, boots soaked from the wet. From behind her she could hear him raging, getting closer.

A beam of dull yellow cut into the forest, bouncing off the trees.

"I will find you!"

In the enclosure of the forest, his voice seemed louder, almost echoing. She sealed her mouth closed to prevent snow from rushing in as she hurried forward, frozen and exhausted. Kelly knew the odds of survival were against her. One moment she thought he was gone, and the next he was closer. She scrambled up an embankment, the snow crunching and sloshing beneath her boots.

Slipping, stumbling, her knees drove into the ground causing her pain and frustration. As Kelly came over a rise, she squinted, pawing at snow stuck to her brow.

What is that? There in the distance was a white dome structure. It stood out from the rest of the boulders and terrain but could have easily been mistaken from a distance as a mound of boulders covered by snow, but it wasn't. Her eyes bounced from it to the lookout looming over the trees. Cautiously Kelly approached. She brushed snow from what appeared to be a huge white camouflage tent, that's when she realized what she was gazing at. It was a ground blind used by hunters in the winter. Had one of the hunters who'd stayed at her lookout left it behind?

No.

Kelly looked back before peering inside. It was dark, too dark for her to see anything. Tearing back the opening, she took out Hank's phone and shone the flashlight inward. The moment the bright light illuminated the contents, her heart sank. It washed over a furry mound in the corner.

Boomer.

Instinctively she rushed in, shining the light on the dog's body.

He'd died from a knife wound.

"No," she muttered dropping to her knees and placing her hands on the dead dog. As she shone the flashlight around the abode, she scrambled back, startled at the sight of a face. It didn't move. Someone was sitting there, frozen, his head slumped to one side, his body covered in… dry blood.

Narrowing her gaze and shining the flashlight over the man's face, she suddenly realized who it was — Ray Harding, one of the forest rangers. He was stripped down to just his underwear — his uniform was missing.

Quickly the pieces fell into place.

Chapter 17

Frozen by shock, Kelly stared at Ray until her eyes shifted with the flashlight toward an area of the blind that had been set up with a long lens camera on a tripod. She scrambled over and put her eye up to the viewfinder.

It was pointing directly at her lookout.

No. Her jaw dropped.

She pressed the button on the camera and a light flashed as it powered on. Kelly switched to the gallery, and a collection of photos that had been recently taken. There were a myriad of images. Many had occurred in the period of time that Erin and Bryce had been there, the rest were of her, alone in the lookout, and then out running with Boomer.

Kelly stepped back, unable to grasp the weight of the situation. He'd been watching, stalking, but only over the past week. Her foot bumped into something, knocking it over. She looked down and found a foldable chair on its side, there beside it was a box full of copies of her book. She picked one up and opened it. There in the front was her signature and a short message signed to Jarod Davis, with a date. She reached for another that had a different message and date but it was made out to the same person. Quickly, she rummaged through the box, opening each cover, one book after the next. All of them were her book, all of the dates corresponded with her book signing tours in different cities. He'd purchased the same book, and got it signed every time.

She looked at the name again. *Jarod Davis.*

Like a light switch turning on, it was beginning to make sense.

"I tried to get your attention," he said from behind her. Kelly whirled around to see Travis in the doorway of the blind. "I was there in the audience at your very first book signing. Don't you remember?" He stepped inside, a strained smile forming. "Of course you do. You smiled at me and kept eye contact throughout your talk. That's when I knew we had a connection, Kelly, something far deeper than the others."

Kelly took a few steps back, her heart racing.

"I hadn't bought your book until that day. In fact if it wasn't for my ex I would haven't even been in that bookstore that afternoon. She wanted me to sign the divorce papers. I was having the worst day, month — hell, year you might say." He smiled, looking away as if recalling. "But you changed that. I was about to leave and find a quiet motel and end it all but then I saw you and that long line of readers waiting to get their copy signed." His smile faded. "There you were in all your glory, smiling and greeting strangers like friends." He paused. "That was the first time I picked up a copy of *A Call to War*. I thumbed through and read the first few pages and I was immediately hooked. It was like you were talking directly to me." He smiled again. "Anyway, I bought a copy that day. The first of many." He chuckled. "It's in the box down there. Do you want to see it?" He took a few steps and she shook her head, backing up.

"It's okay. Kelly. I'm not going to hurt you. I could

never hurt you. You're the only one that understood my pain, the only one that really got me." He thumbed over his shoulder. "That back there, I was just trying to get you to stop running. I wouldn't have hurt you…" She clutched her bloody shoulder showing him that she didn't believe a word he said. "I… I…" he stumbled over his words, a look of despair sinking in, maybe at the thought of losing control. "All I want is for you to listen to me, sit with me, read to me, be with me. We'll be happy together. I know it."

She glanced down at the dog and his gaze followed. "I'm sorry but he would have got in the way. All of them would. I… I couldn't have that. Not again."

"Again?"

He met her gaze. "You really don't remember, do you?" His brow furrowed, a pained expression. "I was at all the signings. I even reached out to you, complimented you on what you were wearing."

She thought back to the flood of emails she'd received. Within the first year there were hundreds, too many to keep track of, too many to have one stand out… but one did. It was always signed with two letters: JD. At first she was flattered. At least initially, the attention from readers was new and unexpected, and it wasn't one or two emails that bothered her. That was normal for anyone chatting with an author but it was the frequency, and then the length. These weren't short, off-the-cuff remarks, like "I'm a fan of your book and I like your writing" emails, no… these weren't the kind that were commonly found in an author's inbox. They were two thousand words long, several times a day, and the expectation to answer persisted.

When she didn't, he would respond asking if she was okay.

As for keeping track of who attended events. Fans were fans, some would travel to multiple events. It was common to see the same face, except his didn't stand out.

"Look, I can understand you not remembering me from the signings." He gave a nervous laugh. "That's because I changed the color of my hair, right? Blond, black, brown, I wore hats, glasses, showed up clean shaven, with a full beard, a mustache… you know… so you wouldn't be freaked out but… even then you looked at me. That's why I thought you knew. I thought we had this inside joke, that you didn't want to tell anyone else. That only you and I were privy to."

She stared back at him with a look of complete astonishment.

"Didn't you get the photos? You must have… the photos of all the books I'd purchased, my library dedicated to you." He glanced down at the box. "Oh, that's just a few. I've got many more at home." His chest rose and fell fast, excited to finally tell her. "I have this beautiful photo of you. From the very first print run. It was taken up near here, right?" He waited for a response but got none. "I just remember the lookout in the background. Not too many like yours." He smiled. "I even sent you photos of me."

He could tell she was bothered by his admission. It was getting worse by the second. Stalkers were common but her agent had protected her from that, sifted through letters, at least she thought so. She couldn't recall getting photos or any letters from JD. That would have definitely been a red flag.

Kelly's eyes bounced to the doorway.

"It bothers me that you don't remember. You should remember. Why don't you remember? I'm not like the others. Those flakes that say they like your work but move on to other books and spend their time going to other signings. I was loyal to you. There was no one else but you."

She nodded, trying to keep him calm as he was still holding Hurst's gun at his side. His finger twitched over the trigger. She could see his breathing had become labored.

"Do you think I can see that first book?" she asked.

He frowned, then gave a look of surprise, maybe joy. "You want to see it?"

"Yeah." She nodded. "Maybe I can read you a chapter from it."

His jaw dropped. "You would do that?"

"Of course. Who else would buy this many books except a true fan?"

He nodded in agreement, flashing his pearly whites. "Oh this, this is fantastic. I promise, Kelly. I will make it up to you. I… I… will clean up this mess and…" He hurried over to the box and fished through it.

Right then Kelly saw her opportunity.

She darted for the door but he must have expected it as he shot toward her, tackling her waist and bringing her down hard. All the air in her lungs expelled as he clawed his way on top of her. "No. No. Stop fighting me."

His hand lashed out and he backhanded her across the face. "Now look what you made me do."

In a flash she was back there, three weeks ago with Cole above her.

It was his face she saw, his words, his angry look of disapproval.

His empty reasons for hurting her. "You're just like all the rest. You really don't care. You want to throw me aside like I'm nothing. Well I won't let you. I won't let you. You hear me!" His voice rose.

Had Travis done this to other authors? It sure as hell seemed like it. He straddled her, forcing his weight down, holding her wrists. "Stop fighting." He slapped her again and she knew if he did it any harder she would go unconscious. Right then, Kelly did the only thing she could and kneed him as hard as she could in the crotch. His eyes bulged and he cried out. She had to do it twice before he released his grip and rolled off. Instantly, she scrambled to her feet, kicking snow out from beneath her as she burst out of the hunter's blind and raced away.

Travis, Jarod, if they were even his names, screamed at her as he unloaded another round.

Kelly ran through the porridge-like snow, following an almost hidden path that would lead her into the national park, toward a ranger station. It was far off but closer than attempting to head toward town. She tried to forget the pain in her knee that was causing her to limp, or the agonizing bloody shoulder wound, but it was excruciating.

The snow bombarded her from every side, attempting to suffocate and slow her down, but she wouldn't let it. She kept moving, trying to outrun the paralyzing drop in temperature. The lake wasn't far, once she had it in sight she would get her bearings and then she could make it to the ranger station.

Wind howled, bringing with it a solid wall of snow.

It was so loud that Kelly didn't hear him until Travis was nearly upon her. When she burst out of the tree line, and made it to the cliff's edge, she knew she'd veered off course. Snow went over, along with several rocks, to the frozen lake below. She glanced back, ready to head into the tree line again and work her way down when Travis appeared, out of breath, holding the gun up at her, preventing escape. "Stop. Just stop. I don't want to hurt you."

She glanced down, her feet inching back toward the ice-covered lake far below. "Stay back. Leave me alone."

"I can't do that."

"I'll jump. I will."

He thrust out a cautious hand. "No, I told you. I don't want to hurt you."

A crack of a gun erupted, then another and Travis' eyes widened and he dropped to his knees, curling. "But I do," a familiar voice said loudly. A hooded figure emerged from the frosted tree line with a rifle. With one hand, he slipped the hood back to reveal his face.

"Cole?" Kelly said.

"Huh! I have to give it to that crazy fucker; he really did outdo himself. What a mess." He smiled taking his eyes off Travis and looking at Kelly, holding the barrel of the rifle low. "And yet it's perfect."

"You put him up to this?" she asked.

He cocked his head. "Not exactly. More like pointed him in your direction. No, this..." He chuckled. "This was all him. You see, I figured he would just screw with your world, freak you out, and make your life a living hell, but this... well... it couldn't be any better if I had planned it out myself." He chuckled again in amusement.

"Why?" she asked.

"Why?" He frowned back at her. Cole unzipped his coat to reveal his full police uniform. "This…" he said pointing to it. "This is all I have and you wanted to take that away from me." He shook his head. "That's not happening."

Kelly put out a hand trying to de-escalate. "Cole. Please."

"No," he bellowed stabbing a finger at her. "You don't get to speak. You've had your say… and it was all lies."

"I didn't lie."

"Oh but you didn't tell the truth either. But don't worry, I will once you're gone." He said it so coldly and matter-of-factly.

"Cole."

"Shut up!" he said taking a few more steps toward her, snapping up and down his hand like a mouth in front of him. "All you do is yak, yak, yak. I'm sick of it." She stepped back and nearly lost her footing. A cold wind blew against her threatening to push her over. "Oh, Kelly the blameless. Never at fault, are you? No, it's all me. You had nothing to do with the way things unfolded, isn't that right? Huh? You were just a helpless writer trying to live out your life with a nasty husband who was jealous." He laughed. "Jealous! That's what you told them, right? That I was jealous of you? You self-righteous bitch! Who covered the cost of everything when you were trying to make something of yourself? Huh? Me. Who had your back when others asked what you were doing with your life? Me. And this is how you repay me?" he said through gritted teeth.

"They'll never believe you."

"Oh, but they will," he said fishing into his jacket pocket and pulling out a handful of envelopes and shaking them in the air. "You know how many celebrities have stalkers? How many have broken into their homes? How many have shown up uninvited? How many have threatened them? The headlines are full of celebrities getting restraining orders." He got closer to her and tossed a few of the envelopes at her feet. They were already open. She bent down and picked them up and fished out the letters, keeping her eyes on Cole. Each one was signed JD, each one written to her, pages and pages of him talking about how they would one day be together, how he couldn't live without her in his life, and how they were meant to be with one another. But that wasn't just it, there were photos of her taken without her knowledge. Photos of her getting into a taxi, ordering coffee, walking down the street, going into her agent's office and going about her private life. She looked up at Cole, almost speechless.

"You told the department I had a stalker, didn't you?"

He smiled and nodded. She was about to learn from her lawyer what Cole's defense was, and what was holding things up, but now she knew.

Cole took a few more steps toward her, his face lighting up. "Pay attention, Kelly, as this is the best part. They'll find him dead, and the people he's killed, and these letters, and a very dead police officer nearby. Based on evidence found they will conclude that Officer Hurst was too late in coming to your aid, but managed to shoot him with his rifle before succumbing to his own injuries," he said holding up the rifle that must have belonged to Hurst. That's when she noticed Cole was wearing gloves. "Like I said, it's perfect. They'll understand that there was truth to my original statement and I will be reinstated and you..." He laughed. "And, you... well, you'll be dead. A tragedy at the hands of an obsessive stalker who couldn't live without the woman he loved." He raised a finger. "Oh, but hold that thought." He crossed over to where Travis was, all the while keeping the rifle trained on her. He reached down and picked up the handgun Travis had been carrying. "Can't be using this," he said tossing the rifle. "I'll bring Hurst over after. Set him beside the rifle and well... have our man here..." He chuckled. "I mean, me, shoot you and that should do it."

Kelly placed both of her hands out in front of her. "Cole, please. You don't have to do this."

"I know. I want to." His expression went dark.

Behind him, Travis moved. He wasn't dead. The

movement was ever so slight only she saw it. Travis raised his gaze at her then at Cole who continued his tirade of abuse as the wind masked Travis' rise.

"Now what was that you said about writing… finish what you started?" Cole slowly lifted the handgun at her. "Goodbye, Kelly."

In a final act of obsessive possession or sacrifice, Travis lunged forward. It all happened in an instant, so fast she could barely process it. He slammed into Cole, wrapping his arms around his waist and thrusting him toward the edge of the cliff. At the same moment, the gun went off. Kelly flinched, thinking she was shot but then opened her eyes in time to see them barreling toward her. She shifted to avoid the collision but Cole snagged her jacket, pulling her backwards with them as they soared over the edge.

Chapter 18

It was like diving into a bath of liquid nitrogen.

Travis took the brunt of the fall, his back cracking the slick sheet of ice. The impact of their combined weight forced them through into the frigid lake water trapped below. Whether expecting to drown, or gasping in shock as she went over the bluff, Kelly had taken a large lungful of air on the way down.

The blast of icy cold water stung like a thousand jellyfish.

Her body convulsed in the sudden shock.

At first she didn't have the wherewithal to even think.

It was dark beneath the ice. Inky black and made even scarier by the sight of Cole. Years of fear immediately took hold, threatening to paralyze her. For a second she saw Travis' body sink into the darkness, his eyes wide, fixed on her, his mouth agape.

You're not dying here. Not here, she told herself.

Kelly's will to survive ignited like an engine growling to life.

Bursting upward she swam a few feet until she felt a hand on her leg.

She kicked her feet to no avail.

Cole had hold of her.

Thrashing in his grip, Kelly tried to swim harder but was quickly pulled down.

As she struggled to break free, he overwhelmed her, his hands finding their target, wrapping around her throat seeking to finish what he'd started. Kelly stared into his eyes, nothing but potholes of darkness and anger reflecting back as she fought for her life. Clumsy winter jackets and heavy boots weighed them down, making even the tiniest movement hard. Her hands wrapped around his wrists, trying to pry them loose, but he was too strong. Every attempt to break free only made him tighten more. They sank deeper; her lungs heaved as they cried for air. It felt like her insides would explode if she didn't catch a breath. Punching, poking, she tried everything but Cole wouldn't let go.

She slammed up against him and they twisted and turned in the murky waters, just two bodies lost in darkness. Her hands fumbled aimlessly, scraping at his duty belt hoping to find anything, a weapon, a gun but it wasn't there. Slowly, darkness crept in at the sides of her eyes. Seconds. That's all it would take. She was moments away from losing consciousness. Groping in the dark, her hand latched on to the knife in his duty belt. Clicking up the button, she felt it come loose.

Cole was so focused on strangling her, he didn't even realize until it was too late.

Kelly thrust the knife up into his rib cage, twice, then pulled it out and watched his face go into shock. Though he was still holding her neck, his grasp weakened and then he fell away, slipping backward, swallowed by the lake.

Bubbles, small and big, escaped her lips as she rose.

How long had she been under?

Seconds, a minute? It was hard to tell.

Overwhelmed, and desperate for air, Kelly sloughed off her jacket, and kicked upward as hard as she could toward the surface. It was so dark she couldn't tell what was up or down until her head slammed into ice. A cold shock of pain went through her skull as she beat on the sheet of ice with her fist but it wouldn't budge. The undercurrent carried her along, pulling and twisting her in its watery grasp.

That's when she took the knife and stabbed the ice; once, twice, three times. Had the current not been as strong she might have been able to focus the tip of the knife on one area but it kept inhaling her backward into its dark mouth. Only capable of making a few cracks at a time before being swept away, she saw darkness creeping in.

Any second.

Any moment now and she would go unconscious.

Kelly dug deep for what little strength remained, hearing Erin's words echoing. *You're stronger than you think.* She slammed the tip of the knife upward using all her strength. Whether the patch of ice was thinner in that spot or her will to survive was stronger, she'd never know — Kelly's fist broke through, cracking it above, a spider web of lines fissured out, weakening the rest and turning the ice into fragments.

One final kick, and her mouth breached the surface, taking in a lungful of air.

Remembering what her father had taught her about how to survive a fall through the ice, Kelly clambered onto the edge of the strongest section. She leaned forward, stabbed the tip of the knife against the ice and used it to gain traction to pull herself up, then began kicking her legs until her body was horizontal. Finally she pulled herself onto her elbows and slid forward on the ice.

Paranoid that it would break again, she lay there for a few seconds until the frigid wind nipped at her skin, threatening to cause hypothermia. She knew the symptoms: slurred speech, confusion, clumsiness, sleepiness, shivering and a weak pulse. Sliding away from the weakest area of ice, still gripped by fear, Kelly cautiously worked her way across the ice as fast as she could. Once she made it to the foot of the cliff, she wrapped her arms around her body and hurried back to the lookout to get warm.

Stumbling through the snow, she could feel her muscles weakening, becoming too cold to function. Kelly collapsed, then got up again, falling forward a few feet later into the snow, her eyes rolling back as she succumbed to the winter. She wasn't sure how long she was there before she heard the voice.

"Over here. Over here!"

A whimper for help escaped her blue lips.

"Ms. Danvers."

The blurred face of a young cop in uniform holding a radio solidified before her before going hazy. "Stay with me. Stay with me!" A radio crackled and she heard him request EMS before looming over and scooping her up. "Help is on the way." The last thing Kelly saw was her snow-covered lookout before everything went black.

Epilogue

A year and a half later

Kelly stabbed the paper with the ballpoint pen before closing the hardcover.

She handed the book back to a grateful reader before turning to her assistant, Tim, and indicating she was ready for that break.

A small white sign to say she would be back in fifteen minutes was posted in front of the desk stacked with copies of her latest novel — *Escaping Darkness.* Barnes & Noble in Boise was busy that Saturday morning as she stepped outside and breathed in the warm summer air. She worked out the tension in her neck from signing over three hundred copies. She set her aviator glasses on and glanced in the display window where her book was front and center, surrounded by multiple copies.

It almost looked like a shrine.

She couldn't help but think of Jarod, aka Travis, and that box, or what he'd told her about his private library or shrine dedicated to her.

In the weeks following that cold winter night when many lost their lives, she'd come to learn that she wasn't the first to have crossed paths with Jarod Davis. He'd had multiple restraining orders, had done six months in jail for breaking into another author's home, and had narrowly escaped a lengthy sentence for stalking.

Though he was unable to speak for himself, media outlets were quick to theorize why he'd done it. She and two authors before her were similar in appearance to his ex-wife, a woman who had scorned him and walked out taking his kids with her. A woman who later came forward to make a few bucks off her story about living with a controlling monster. Viewers ate it up, and Kelly had already been approached by one director about turning her time at the lookout with Jarod into a film, but she'd turned it down, saying that living through it once was enough for her.

She pushed the thought of him from her mind.

As for Cole, well, that was a whole other kettle of fish. He was as equally controlling and demented as JD. He wasn't lying when he said he'd directed Jarod toward Kelly. After an extensive investigation it was determined that it wasn't Nora filtering her mail, it was Cole. Attempting to control her life, Cole had taken the mail arriving at the house, and had seen the endless stream of bizarre letters from Jarod, from there it was simply a matter of pointing him in her direction. No different than a jilted security guard of a gated community giving the access code out to a stalker. After the night she went to the police, it was concluded that Cole had replied to JD, under the guise that it was Kelly responding. Multiple letters were found at Jarod's residence in Boise. The handwriting was a match for Cole's. While Cole hadn't directly told him to come to the lookout, he'd given him enough rope to hang himself: information that she was back in town (gained from someone who had spoken with

Erin prior to her arrival), news that she was working on a new book, but most importantly, he'd listed the lookout's location at the top of the letter.

From there it was just a matter of time before Jarod showed up in Emery.

Kelly sighed. So many good people had lost their life because of Cole. Sure, Jarod had been the one to take those lives but Cole had directed his actions. As for Erin and Hank, well, their bodies were found and in light of the situation, the court deemed Hank's death an accident.

Still, it wasn't easy to live with and Kelly was seeing a therapist to work through it all.

However, even as the months passed and the sting of loss grew less painful, there were moments when she wondered if there were other fans like JD out there, ready to step in and take his place.

"Oh wow, you're Kelly Danvers, aren't you?" a woman asked coming up behind her. An awkward feeling rose, that uncomfortable moment that came with her career.

She cleared her throat. "That's right."

The lady looked overjoyed, her husband not so. The woman asked if she could take a selfie before gushing over Kelly's latest book and telling her how it was the best thing since sliced bread and how she intended to wait in line to have her copy personally autographed. Kelly let her take the photo, thanked her and walked a short distance away, hoping to avoid any further attention. Since the event her agent had been nagging at her to restrict the amount of access readers had through her website, social media and book tours, but Kelly shot it down. In her mind, doing so would give JD a foothold in her life and if she was to live out a normal existence, she wanted to act normal, and stay connected with readers. After all, it was them who had given her a career.

And for that she was grateful. Genuinely, even if she was an introvert.

The lot around the bookstore that morning was packed with vehicles. Many were out getting their weekend shopping or simply basking in the soaring temperature.

It felt good to feel the sunshine on her skin.

Kelly reached into her bag and checked the messages on her phone from her mother. There was one: *I didn't want to disturb you. I know you're busy, honey, call me when you get a moment.*

She dialed, stretching out her back as she waited for her mother to pick up.

"Hi darling."

"Hey."

"How's it going?"

"Good. Two more cities after this and I should get a break and be home."

She was now staying only a few blocks from her mother in the city. She'd bought a cute place, a small two-bedroom house, nothing fancy, modest, something that allowed for growth if she ever decided to have a family. Her mother wanted her to move in but she still wanted her independence and Kelly was only walking distance away if she wanted to drop in.

"Heard any more news?"

"Yeah, looks like I have a buyer," Kelly said, enthusiastically.

Although she loved the lookout, and was previously against the idea of selling it — the place was now mired in intense grief and memories that she preferred to forget. With Hank gone, she'd posted it with the Fire Lookout Association, an organization that was involved in the research and preservation of current and former fire lookouts. They'd offered her a listing on their website and within a week she had multiple offers from people who had a genuine interest in its history and preservation, not simply because of the murders.

"That's good news." There was a pause. "You doing okay?"

Her mother checked in regularly just to be sure.

"Yeah. I'm good. How's Megan?"

"She's well, I'm with the baby as I speak. You really have to see her, Kelly. She has Adam's eyes."

A pause.

"Someday."

"Kelly. Megan wants you to see her."

Even though she couldn't have prevented their deaths, Kelly couldn't help but feel guilty. It was because of that she'd decided to donate the earnings from her second novel to Megan and her child, and the families of Erin, Hank, and Officer Hurst to ensure they didn't want for anything. And, well, she still made enough money from her first book to live comfortably with close to a million copies sold worldwide every year.

Her assistant called out to her and tapped his watch.

"Listen, Mom, sorry to cut you short but I have to go. I will be in touch in a couple of days. I promise. Love you."

After she returned to the table, a long line of people were waiting. "Thanks for your patience, everyone." She took a seat and began the rewarding but repetitive task of signing books and greeting each person. After seeing numerous copies of her latest novel pass in front of her, it caught her off guard when a fresh hardcover of *A Call to War* slid before her.

THE LOOKOUT: A Gripping Survival Thriller

She lifted her eyes, to see a clean-shaven, middle-aged man, dark eyes, good looking. He wore a long tweed jacket, and a jean shirt tucked into stylish gray pants.

He smiled but said nothing.

Kelly stared down at the book. It had been a long time since she'd signed one of these. "Huh? Do you want the latest signed too? Or just this?"

"Just that one," he replied politely.

She nodded slowly, and opened the front. "Who do I make it out to?"

"JD."

Her stomach sank and went into knots and she began having a coughing fit. Tim stepped in and offered a bottle of water. Kelly took a giant gulp and breathed out again. "You okay?" Tim asked placing a reassuring hand on her shoulder.

She waved him off. "Yeah, yeah, good. Must have had something stuck in my throat." She looked at the man in line. "My apologies," she said.

Her hand trembled slightly as she scrawled a short and

general message, thanking JD for the support. She closed it and handed it back. He thanked her and went to walk away. "JD. What's that short for?" she asked.

The man cast a glance over his shoulder. "Jennifer Decker."

"Oh," she replied, breaking into a smile. Her fears subsided. "So it's not for you?"

He returned to the table. "No, it's a gift for my sister. She's not well so I said I would come and get it signed for her."

Kelly smiled. "That's very thoughtful. So you haven't read it, yourself?"

He grimaced and looked around and then leaned in and whispered. "No. I haven't. No offense, but uh… it's really not my kind of genre. I'm more into sci-fi."

With that she burst out laughing and he smiled back.

She wagged her finger at him as she took a book from the next person in line.

"Honesty. I like that."

And just like that the guy melted back into the crowd,

just another face, just another reader, but fortunately, this time... not a fan.

* * *

THANK YOU FOR READING

If you enjoyed that, check out Rules of Survival or Days of Panic. Please take a second now to leave a review. Even a few words is really appreciated. Thanks kindly, Jack.

About the Author

Jack Hunt is the author of horror, sci-fi and post-apocalyptic novels. He currently has over thirty books published. Jack lives on the East coast of North America. If you haven't joined Jack Hunt's Private Facebook Group you can request to join by going here. https://www.facebook.com/groups/1620726054688731/ This gives readers a way to chat with Jack, see cover reveals, and stay updated on upcoming releases. There is also his main Facebook page if you want to browse that.

www.jackhuntbooks.com
jhuntauthor@gmail.com